SALT-STUNG ON CAPE HATTERAS
CAPE POINTE BOOK 1

By Cindy M. Amos

Copyright © 2021 by Cindy M. Amos
Published by Forget Me Not Romances, an imprint of Winged Publications

This book is a work of fiction. Names, characters, places, and incidents are the product of the author's imagination and are used fictitiously. Any resemblance to actual events, locales, or persons, living or dead, is coincidental.

All rights reserved including the right to reproduce this book or portions thereof in any form whatsoever – except short passages for reviews – without express permission.

ISBN: 9798509957819

New Hanover County Public Library
201 Chestnut St.
Wilmington, NC 28401

*Far above the roar of the ocean,
mightier than its thundering breakers
stands the Lord on heaven's heights.
His testimony will never alter
though the sands shift down below.
Psalm 93:4-5*

Dedicated to
The fishermen sinking bottom rigs along
Hatteras pointe

Acknowledgments
Cameron H. Amos, Original Cover Design
Cynthia Hickey, Winged Publications
Stacey Rogers, Trinity Social Media

CHAPTER 1

The shoals running off cape pointe sucked the life out of terra firma, but no one ever came to Hatteras to gawk at underwater elevations. No, Jaima Delarie knew better. They came to fish. October ramped up angler excitability. Bluefish would start running the inlet any day now.

With the tide ebbing, the ocean pulled at her ankles as if to insist on her departure. One glance at the two shrimp left in her bait box argued against that brash tactic. Unfortunately, those thawing crustaceans would keep her brooding out in the intertidal zone through dead slack tide, most likely. If that yielded her one fresh fish to cook for dinner tonight, she could justify the time. *C'mon. One measly Spanish mackerel, Lord.*

The daring peninsula of sand chopped the oceanic currents like atmospheric turbulence battling for supremacy. Rising tide quelled the aqueous fight to encompass dry land, but an ebb tide lacked strength to sort out such matters. Her life had taken on the illusion of a falling tide lately. She reeled in her line to find her leader affixed with a dangling triangular weight and a bare hook. "Minus one shrimp and counting."

As she baited the hook, a powder-blue motorboat passed heading inland. The crossing of Pamlico Sound took the better part of half an hour, even under mild winds. The channel markers would be blinking back darkness by then. Anguished at not having caught dinner, she wiped her hand dry and cocked the surf rod back to cast.

Instinctive, she checked the pole's tip for a fouled line and caught a glimpse of the iconic Hatteras lighthouse, its shadow marking the dunes like a sundial. She let the cast rip from the strength of her shoulders. Told she bore a sturdy build by those who knew her best, she put her six-foot frame to work and cleared the shore break by twice the needed distance. A positive sign, the shrimp stayed connected to the bottom rig and made the plunge into the salty Atlantic.

The following lull snapped on a seagull's cry and an odd throttling noise that ended in a hollow thump. A scan of the eastern shoreline yielded one slightly imperiled vessel listing to port and badly aligned for an emergency landing. No one in their right mind beached a watercraft along the shore, as ocean waves could swamp any rookie attempts at dry-land safety. To prove the point, a rolling swell crested against the bow of the boat, an enticing lick of disaster.

Her pulse elevating, she shoved the handle of the fishing pole into the nearby rod holder and sidestepped like a scuttling crab toward the disabled craft. The throttle noise repeated, followed by a metallic clank. When the boat captain threw his arms over his head, the icy drip of peril seized her chest. *Graveyard of the Atlantic repeats its claim.*

Underpowered to manually prevent the landing, she reasoned the last dune buggy had left the beach almost an hour ago. Maybe they should attempt to minimize the damage. She cupped her hands around her mouth to amplify her message and feign a steady calm. "Can you throw your anchor and drag a line to slow down?"

"Dragging two anchors already," the captain replied. "I'm jettisoning cargo. Watch for it." A swell passed, crowning as it approached shore. Two red coolers soon bobbed in the gray-blue waters. Buoyant, they floated in when the next wave crashed onto the wreck scene.

Despite the resisting anchors, all else seemed to morph from impossible rescue to imminent salvage. Jaima drew her cell phone and pressed a familiar number for help. When the line opened, she made it quick. "I've got a boat in peril off cape pointe. She's coming in and nothing's gonna stop that collision. Can you bring the Suburban over?"

"Be right there," a brusque voice replied. "You save the captain—I'll get the boat."

She shirked out of her windbreaker, knotted the sleeves around her phone, and tossed it onto the upper shore for safekeeping. "Sure, give me the easy-breezy job." One glance at her stock-still rod yielded no further excuses. She had to lend aid.

Within seconds, the first cooler rode a breaker into the shallows, so she waded out to retrieve it.

Riding low in the rushing water, she figured fish weighed the box, suggesting the captain might not be a total incompetent. The drag to shore strained her back muscles, but she bent her knees and gave the effort all she had. A repeat trip for the matching cooler proved equally arduous. She rested above the wrack line left by the earlier high tide and watched the captain toss the last of several smaller bundles into the ocean.

A cataclysmic battle ensued between twin-rigged anchors and Mother Nature. The vessel's stern soon became ill-matched for the tidal influence of the moon's gravitational pull. A large swell crested directly into the boat and emptied. Doomed, the craft sunk to half-mast.

A growl emanated from atop the far gunwalc as the captain refused to go down with the ship. In a splash, the Atlantic swallowed the man whole. Its salt-gray waters turned murderous.

Jaima scanned the beachfront from the rolling swells to the shore break. The barrier islands of North Carolina wore the rescue of imperiled ships like a badge of folklore courage. Unfolding in live action, the perilous scene felt more like a tourniquet tightening around her throat. Twice she spotted a dark-haired crown in the surface chop, only to lose sight of the floundering man in the next frothy wave.

A handful of breakers swamped the boat, and its hull began scraping the sandy bottom. Kept from going broadside to the surf, the twin dragging anchors saved the boat, a fated twist of seamanship that kept the barrage of waves from outright demolishing the small vessel.

When a horn sounded from the dune crossing, her rescuer's trip from Hatteras bight came full circle back to cape pointe. Only partially relieved, she crouched in the shallows to minimize the setting sun's glare and tried to locate the victim while the Labrador Current chilled her legs. A dash of plaid shimmered close by, so she trotted out for immediate retrieval. Waiting out the next crashing wave, she waded deeper and squinted to remedy refraction at the water's surface. This time when she spotted plaid, she lunged to make a frantic grab and connected.

A Herculean grasp responded to her touch as a roller broke with a roar. Enveloped in saltwater spray, his arms clutched her trunk and two figures became one under the wave's thunderous christening. Toppled by the wave's power, a confused sense of uprightness gave way to a flushing tumble toward shore. A mix of sand, icy water, and sea foam further convoluted her senses. Deprived of air, her lungs began to burn. At last the waters receded, allowing the upper shore to win.

Monte squatted over them with a belly-shaking chuckle. "That there's one way to land 'em, missy. Let's get the boat out before it fills up with sand and strains my wench. Can one of you castaways find your land legs?"

A pair of mesmerizing hazel eyes shot open at the mention of the boat. His hand rubbed a plaster of wet sand off a tanned cheek. "Lord on earth. What just happened?"

She shoved out of his clasping arm and rolled

back to retake her feet. In a squat, she regarded the wreck-prone captain as water dripped from her jeans. "You just missed Hatteras Inlet by approximately two hundred feet."

He moaned and tried to sit upright in the sand. "Not sure if I ran out of gas or the engine failed. Either way, a miss is as good as a shipwrecked mile."

Monte pointed at him. "You come up front and help keep the bow centered on the rollers. Del-doll, you take the bailer and rid excess weight from the hull as best you can." He tossed her the scoop and made for the cab of the Suburban.

Jaima walked out on wet sand exposed by a dead slack tide and rued the happenstance. Bailing the almighty Atlantic out of a skiff's hull stacked the deck toward impossible yet again. Behind the sulking hull, two taut anchor lines trailed seaward like contrails tracing some ill-chosen path. *The men can fetch those tethered beasts.* With a heave of her shoulders, the first scoop of sand and water regained its home off cape pointe.

~

Perry looked across the kitchen table and read the no-nonsense look in his brother's eyes. A Manning had lived in this modest house for a century and a half, though he foundered lately to keep the heritage alive. "Think of some other way to make money. We have a month of fishing left, at most. Now we're down one boat. It's gonna take all winter to refurbish mine. Between the two of us, we need to come up with a profitable scheme."

Dalton shrugged. "My family finances are

covered, thanks to Beth's dietician job over at the senior care home. If we have a humble Christmas, we don't need much extra money."

He intensified his stare. "That's what you said last year, and my nephews had a pretty slim Christmas. We need to get the new guide business going. I'll work on the flyer tonight. We may gain some interest at the RV show in New Bern. Let me check into that vendor booth cost."

"Suit yourself. If we both book fishing outings this winter, then you'd better get dad's boat fixed."

"Yeah—with the stack of invisible money just waiting outside my reach. Thanks for your helpful insights. In a pinch, I could borrow Uncle Glenn's boat."

Dalton stood, making the chair scrape the floor. "Count on me to pull my weight out on Pamlico Sound. No worries. Grandpa taught us all the fishing holes between here and Stumpy Point." He centered the back of his hand in front of eyes and faked a grin. "All too familiar."

"Exactly what I thought until the boat motor sputtered and tried to end my last fishing trip in catastrophe." He rose to follow Dalton to the door.

"Come over tomorrow and let me take a gander at your sales flyer."

He swallowed the caustic comeback that floated to mind while the transom of his salvaged boat glided down the gravel drive like a magic trick. "Hey. Monte's delivering my boat. What a nice guy." He passed Dalton in the doorway, settling his favorite fishing hat in place. This delivery would save him valuable time, not to mention gas. He'd have to thank the old salt for his generous initiative.

Dalton flanked the vintage Suburban and headed for the passenger-side window. After taking a peek, he straightened with a look of astonishment on his face. With a hand clamped across his mouth, he retreated across the driveway to his house next door.

Undeterred, Perry approached the driver's window as the glass cranked down. His pretty rescuer sat inside. *Wow—talk about an outright blessing.* After leaving her a mackerel that fated day, he hadn't gotten a chance to express his gratitude. "Well, if it isn't Ms. Del-doll. I'll be."

She snickered. "My real name is Jaima Delarie. Only Monte gets to call me Del-doll, and half the time he doesn't really mean it as a term of affection."

"First, nice job backing in the boat. Second, how on earth did you find me?"

She produced a wallet that creaked open with stiffened leather. "I combed the beach until nightfall made it too hard to see, but I managed to salvage some of your packages. Fourteen Back Sound Drive didn't prove too tough to find—once I sniffed my way to Belhaven."

"Ah, the sulfur salt marsh smell. Like salt spray and sand in your sheets, it's just one more coastal perk a person learns to endure. Hey, if you have time, I can show you around. We have a dock on Pantego Creek that leads out to the Pungo River."

"Sure, I'd like the tour. Plus, I promised Monte that I would cool the engine at least an hour before heading back to Manteo. Belhaven falls a little outside of his normal range."

To hide his pleasure, he darted to the vehicle's rear bumper and made quick work of unhitching the trailer. A host of bumper stickers touted the local fishing industry, but he favored the pink crustaceans on the crab spawning sanctuary sticker the most. Sensing Monte might make a good connector to possible tour gigs in the Hatteras area, he'd have to take him a flyer and ask for client referrals. As for Monte's substitute today, the right angle remained unclear.

Maybe that's why Dalton looked so stupefied. If Beth hadn't acted on what she wanted, he might not have any nephews by now. Manning men approached romance like fish swimming toward a seine net, wide-eyed and unaware. He cranked the trailer's jack down and straightened to find a tall, slender woman by his side. Dressed in an open-weave sweater the color lining a conch shell, her light brown hair mesmerized him for a dull-witted second.

She tipped down her sunglasses. "I have the other packages in the back floorboard, all dried out. Rest assured your first aid kit is ready to embark on the high seas again."

He laughed at her tease. "Yeah, well. That gauze will sure come in handy if I need some extra salt to clean a wound. Let's stroll back to the dock."

"Looks like you might not be the first salt-stung victim here. Was this your dad's?"

"Yeah, and his father before that. We all fished for a living, but I'm the only one who can claim being shipwrecked on Hatteras. The wiser men going before me respected that ominous marker and steered clear." He tossed an empty oil can toward the garage and wondered why the yard appeared so cluttered. In such hot pursuit of a sustaining income, he'd grown a bit blind to keeping the place neat. That landed with a twinge of regret today for some reason.

"Who peeped in on me back there?"

"My brother Dalton who lives next door. He bought Aunt Sally's house. It's convenient so we can both use the family dock. He's my fishing partner."

The mown path down to the dock narrowed, putting them shoulder to shoulder. He watched a pair of dragonflies dance in the air before thinking clear enough. "This is a bit overdue, but thank you for pulling me out of the water the day I crashed the boat onto shore. I recall being a little shell-shocked afterward, but I wanted you to know how much I appreciate the rescue. Maybe leaving you a mackerel didn't fully express my sentiments."

"No regrets. I needed that fish." A slight smile chased the comment. "I ran light on grocery money because I had to pay a one-time maintenance fee at my apartment complex in Manteo, so that fish fed me three days. I should be thanking you."

He nodded. "Farmers and fishermen feed the world. Not only do I truly believe that truth, I live it every day. God gave me a black thumb for growing plants, so I stick with the fishing part." He gestured to the planked dock and led her onto its broad width. "Here's our attempt to suspend gravity over Pantego Creek. From here, I can make Pamlico

Sound in ten minutes."

Jaima scanned the dock. "Oh, what a great double kayak. Want to take me out?"

"Sure. Sounds like a perfect way to cool an overheated engine." While reaching for two oars, he sensed a fine-mesh net strung up ahead. From the kayak's stern, he'd stay plenty ready to duck any menacing entanglement.

Chapter 2

Jaima figured a nor'easter would take out the humble hut some day, but until then she'd frequent the weathered doorstep and hope that somehow counted as righteousness. Easily the oldest resident on the island, Edwina Creef deserved her respect—and possibly—more frequent visits. Odder than a duck-billed platypus, Edwina had her own way of living which didn't include much fussing over hygiene, especially where she excelled—the kitchen.

No one had ever died from rancid oil boiling in Edwina's deep fat fryer, so who was she to tempt fate? With few cans in her own picked-over pantry, she would welcome any handouts that might transpire. She glanced over at Monte's house across the way and tried to recall exactly how those two claimed kinship. The tie came through Monte's war hero father, as best she could remember. She struck her knuckles across the weathered wood framing the door and waited.

The sound of bare feet shuffling across the floor announced the occupant. "Lord to kill me if it ain't our 'quarium girl. You been too busy to come see me lately?" She shoved the screen door with her palm and it squawked open.

"Pretty busy. The university wants that wet lab to raise horseshoe crabs up and running by the year's end. Too bad the crabs don't like living at the aquarium."

The senior resident laughed and showed off all four of her remaining teeth. "No, I reckon those critters belong off Hatteras bight where the Good Lord sowed 'em. Come in and sit a spell. Goodness, the air's got chilly out here."

"Yes, it finally feels like October." She stepped into the cottage's dark interior where everything bore at least one layer of hand-stitched slipcovers, if not two. "I really came over to see if I could collect your trash. They just emptied the dumpster at the apartment so I have lots of room to sneak in your contribution."

Edwina chuckled while lowering into her regular perch, a wooden rocker that wore a tufted pink cushion to pad her skinny frame. "That's our little secret. Tell me what you've been up to lately. Caught any good fish?"

She sat on the sagging sofa's edge and clamped her arms around her knees. "No, I haven't been highly successful in that department. I did catch a good fisherman of questionable seamanship since he ran his boat aground out on cape pointe last week."

A pleasurable growl worked its way up the woman's throat. "Ha—you mean good-looking fisherman. Monte told me all about it, how flustered you got when the waves tossed you both ashore locked up tighter than two halves of a clam shell. Have you seen the man since?"

"Yes, thanks to Monte's matchmaking efforts. He asked me to drive the wrecked boat out to Belhaven. That's where Perry Manning, the faltering fisherman, lives. They have a dock out back, so he took me kayaking on Pantego Creek. It's pretty back there, so quiet and serene."

"My momma used to talk about movin' inland. We lived at Buxton until I was twelve. Said she got tired of hearing the ocean slap the land's edge, so they moved to the sound side where daddy could catch more shrimp. His people harkened from Currituck County."

"Mainlanders then, I suppose."

"Yep. That sandy soil ain't good for much, but they farmed and made the best of it. Grandpa helped build the Wright Brothers memorial where there won't nothin' but sand up in Kitty Hawk. They used mule teams and pulled the sand into a hill with sleds. One day while he sat in the shade eating fig preserves right out of the jar, I asked him about his meet-up with history. Grandpa claimed the federal government never paid them one red cent for all that hard work. Such a cryin' shame, and his mule team almost fell anemic from all that sand haulin'. That just ain't right to cheat a hired man out of payment he deserves."

She shook her head. "One time my preacher told the congregation not to wait around for life to be fair. Circumstances might not treat us straight-up fair, but it's how we deal with what comes our way that matters more. I hope that failure to get paid didn't make your grandpa bitter about life."

"No, girl. He was a content man, especially if granny cooked him some flounder. I can hardly eat a pan-fried flounder without thinking of those two. Finally, the ocean wore them plum out and salt spray stole their last breath. They passed away within a week of one another, both at low tide. Daddy insisted they be buried at low tide, too, which put us at the cemetery near nightfall. Aunt Gussie carried a lantern, and we kids just followed her with our eyes bugged out trying to keep our feet on the path."

Sensing her host had grown short-winded, she rose. "How about I knock around and collect your trash? If you can find one big bag, we can fit it all together."

"Bring the trash from the bathroom. I'll head out back to the garbage can. I sure hope those festering fish heads aren't gonna make your car stink."

Jaima swallowed down her objection and headed for the only restroom in the tiny house. After all, acts of service shouldn't come predicated on what smelled good. All forfeitures held a taint of some sort, though few delivered a stench worse than rotting fish parts. On quick assessment, she wet a tissue and wiped down the sink, regretting she hadn't brought along some disinfectant. Edwina didn't like her meddling too much, so she dashed around to do what good she could manage in the blink of an eye. A bony white cat met her at the back door. "There's not much here. Did you already empty the kitchen can?"

"Yep, had to yesterday when I burned my first batch of hushpuppies. The second batch turned out fine, though. I saved some in a bread bag, if you'll take a few home."

"I never refuse your cooking. Let me get this stowed in the car while you go get those hushpuppies—after you wash your hands, of course."

She flexed her vein-streaked hands about shoulder height. "Always gagging at gnats and swallowing flies. My momma didn't raise a heathen, girl. I know to clean up first."

Jaima clutched the throat of the bag without letting the fish essence escape. She poured the tissue trash inside and knotted the whole works while heading for the curb. After slamming the hatch shut, she sauntered back up the broken sidewalk to save the old woman a few steps.

Edwina appeared on the porch, the handout waggling in her grip. "I sure enough appreciate you stopping by. Take these but don't eat them 'til suppertime. That way, I'll know you'll sleep sound tonight 'cause of me."

"Thanks so much. I may have to swing by the grocery store later and get something to go with these lumps of cornmeal goodness." She took the baggie and pretended it weighed a ton.

"Watch out for that shipwrecked fisherman you mentioned. It takes a smart girl to know when a fella's navigation might be a tad off-kilter." She tapped her head as if to drive her inference home.

"A smart girl always catches her own fish, Miss Creef. Stay well until I see you next time." She gave her a childish wave and headed for the car. Lighthearted, she tried not to think about the fieldwork waiting up in Salvo. As she recalled, the ocean slapped the shore quite constantly along that stretch of beach. According to Creef wisdom, that could rightly wear a person out. Maybe she could try wearing ear plugs, since the ghost crabs wouldn't mind one bit. Plus, if she grabbed her surf rod beforehand to test the waters for a fish, she might not need to stop at the grocery store.

~

With a glossy new flyer in hand, Perry approached the message board at Full Sails Marina to leave his marketing token. Given their prime location at Whalebone Junction, this pair of enterprising brothers had done quite well for themselves. Mostly catering to pleasure crafts, he knew a similar sidetrack wouldn't befall the Mannings. No, they had to stay focused on fishing.

A man with a double mission today, he'd decided to hit these distribution spots on the perimeter of his target area once he called the aquarium and found out Jaima Delarie had signed out to Salvo for an afternoon of fieldwork. Why he felt the need to drop a bobber into her blue-eyed pond he couldn't reason, except he'd relived that shared hour in the kayak along Pantego Creek at least a dozen times over the past week. Talk about an unreachable itch.

The sputter of an outboard motor chopped into his reminiscing. An open-hulled vessel bearing royal blue and orange markings slid by, the crew scanning the adjoining parking lot like they'd lost something on land. The guy at the helm did a double-take when their gazes collided, but eased along toward the causeway. The transom of the stern bore the name *Agua Aid*. He recognized the name as a start-up rescue company, a pesky remora feeding off the big shark Sea Salvage that took calls straight from the Coast Guard for towing disabled watercraft.

He pulled back the plastic cover and shifted the flyer against the corkboard. Lacking a fastener, he stole the pushpin from a yellowed business card and let it flutter to the pavement. Once level, he closed the Plexiglas and stared at the photo of Dalton holding the catch from a successful tour last summer, a wallop of marine life dangling from a cable. "Reel 'em in, brother. We need the business."

The drive down to mile marker forty-nine lengthened into a blur. Only the aroma of hot dogs he'd stashed in a soft-side cooler kept him aware of the windswept scenery. The sea oats combed the sky with regularity along this stretch, speaking of well-placed preservation. The turnoff for public parking opened up with a weathered sign marking Salvo's existence on the map. With only one vehicle in the lot, Jaima's SUV stood out like a private invitation. He pulled in beside the aquarium's emblem and cut the engine. "Well, here goes nothing." Thinking she might not be hungry yet, his stopover had all the heft of a bottom rig with only hot dogs for bait.

The sand crunched under his deck shoes as he hastened up the dune crossover to gain the shore. Against a panorama of banded ocean blue, he found a solitary beachcomber, bent as if collecting seashells from the wave's edge. When she stood and bent again, he realized she'd taken a measurement. "Ahoy there, Del-doll. How about some company?"

She repeated the surface work and stopped to scribble something in a tiny bound book resting on her hip. When he approached, she pocketed the book and tossed her hair over one shoulder. "Hey there, Belhaven. How's it going?"

"Oh, fair to partly cloudy. I'm just puttering around the Manteo area posting flyers for the Manning Brothers Fish Tours. I wanted to stop by and place one at the aquarium, but when I called, they said you were out on the shore at Salvo—so here I am."

"I just finished my last transect. Now, we can let the ghost crabs continue with life uninterrupted and allow dusk to fall peacefully all around." The roar of a breaker smashing the intertidal zone seemed to override her comment. "Okay, in relative peace anyway."

"Are you hungry yet? I hit my favorite hot dog vendor on the way across Whalebone Junction." He held the bait within striking distance.

"Wow. I don't see how I can say no to that offer. I meant to start fishing by now, but the ghost crab population has been expanding in these parts so work kept me plenty busy."

"Have I walked into your crab census? I must have counted a hundred holes on my way down."

"That's one thousand six hundred and forty-two measured and documented ghost crab burrows. I'm interested to see how much the median size has grown this late in the season. By comparison, the beach at cape pointe boasts a population only half this size."

He tilted his head, unsure what she meant. "Because Hatteras is further south?"

"No, these beaches are fairly comparable habitats and close by one another, so in theory they should host similar ghost crab numbers. I'm using Salvo as my control beach, because it's missing one impact that Hatteras suffers from considerably."

"Would that be manic fishermen?"

"No, Mr. Shipwrecked, but you're close. Would you like to sit beside me on that driftwood log down the beach so we can eat?"

"Sure thing. In the summertime, you can't find a parking spot at this beach access, so I know Salvo gets the foot traffic most crabs hate." He fell into step with her as the slope grew firm with wave-packed sand. Another cresting wave pounded the surf zone, sending up a splashing froth of salt spray and foam.

She scraped off a row of gooseneck barnacles from the sodden log with her shoe and sat, making the logbook protrude from her pocket. "If the manic fishermen of Cape Hatteras would walk out like beachgoers, the crabs would have fewer problems. However, fishermen have gear—and lots of clout. The park service allows the historic use of vehicles to continue at cape pointe, though research can prove driving off-road changes the natural environment."

He sat down an arm's length away

contemplating the tiny beach inhabitant in a sandy world of crisscrossed tire ruts made by street-weight vehicles. The odds stacked against the flimsy crustacean, for sure. "But we don't drive up in the dunes. Maybe they can stay safe by living up there."

She reached for the cooler, found wipes in the outer pocket, and began to clean her hands. "I plan to look at the spatial distribution next. You're right. The full story won't simply be a numbers game. I've casually observed larger burrows up in stands of sea oats on cape pointe, but laying out a grid to map it will prove if any upslope displacement has truly taken place."

He removed his hat and rubbed a hand over his hairline to smooth out a case of prickles. "Some of this stuff we thought might be going on just gets shoved under the mat because we're so determined to hit the beach to fish. That indifference should shame a man—especially one that really cares about nature."

She handed him the wipe and unzipped the bag to claim the top hot dog. "What else have you casually observed today as a grounded boater, Mr. Manning?"

He cleaned his hands and crushed the wipe into his shirt pocket. That earned him a hot dog delivery. "Well, for one thing, those brothers at Full Sails Marina are doing some knockout business. I didn't see an empty slip along their docks. That's what I call steady income."

"Thank you, God, for this little morsel. Amen." She bit into her hot dog and hummed.

He unwrapped his hot dog and brought it to

within striking distance. "I also observed an Agua Aid boat scouting the marina. Who knows what they hunted for?" He took a giant bite and couldn't taste any condiments, a momentary disappointment.

"A broken-down boat, most likely. Hey, I see mustard packets in here. Want some?"

He held out a hand and soon received a portion. After tearing the packet with his teeth, he drizzled mustard down the gap in the bun. "Let's have a few of those fries, too."

"I would call you captain and follow your commanding orders, but the last person who referred to you in that regard hinted your navigation system might be off-kilter."

The tease in her tone made him laugh. A french fry took full advantage and flew into his open gape. The saltiness matched the beachfront to perfection. His enjoyment grew, mostly due to his alluring companion. Maybe if he delved into her studies, he could find out more about her, too. "So, do you frequent washed-up logs with off-kilter men you barely know?"

She paused the stump of her hot dog at her lips as a smile eased her expression. "No, most of the men in my life are stodgily academic types. At the aquarium we primarily deal with universities and medical research facilities. We have what they want—marine invertebrates—so we never have to play the pushover." The gleam of confidence in her eyes echoed that truth.

He felt a nudge to share something personal so he relented. "The aquarium is a great family attraction, too. I'm a big believer in spending time together. That's one reason why the Manning family tends to cluster. I see a lot more of my two nephews by living next door than I would otherwise."

She nodded and waved a bent fry through the air. "Talk about a pushover, Uncle Perry. Tell me their names and something that makes each boy special."

"I'll start with Garrett, the oldest. He changed my life the day he was born when my brother let me hold him. He's eight now, smiling like a croc with a missing front tooth, and already smart about being out on the water. When I told him I wrecked dad's boat on cape pointe, he wouldn't speak to me for two days. See, I'd been tied to the whipping post long before your off-kilter comment landed."

She kicked off her shoes before crossing her ankles. "What about the youngest boy?"

"That's Gavin, and at six years old he's still a momma's boy. He's scared of just about everything at first meet-up. It took him months to get accustomed to the family's new dog. His strong point is drawing, and he always has a pencil nearby to make a sketch. He drew me the old boat dock for my Christmas present. I framed that drawing and hung it over my desk."

"What about that skinny cat I saw stalking around the dock?"

"Garrett named him Sea Foam. The fishing dock always hosts a couple of cats. We clean the fish and toss the innards into the shallows along with the heads. Those cats aren't too proud to go wading in for the pieces they want. In the winter months, Beth lets the boys leave some dry food out on the back deck."

She dug her toes into the sand. "Who's Beth?"

He grabbed the cooler and crammed his wrapper inside. Finding a stray french fry, he let her question hang in the air a few extra seconds. "My brother Dalton married Beth almost nine years ago. Barely twenty years old, I feared he might have made an early mistake, but Beth has been good as gold for him. She works as a dietician at Belhaven Manor, a senior living facility. Her income keeps them anchored, which helps when the fishing business fluctuates."

"So much for the old wives' tale that says the eldest must marry first." She gave him a knowing look. "My kid sister got married four years ago. Believe me, I get tired of the family goading me to follow in her saintly steps."

He pulled the zipper closed, maybe a little too hard. "With a handful of my high school buddies already divorced and crimped with regrets, I'm hiding like your skittish ghost crab friends up in the dunes." When she glanced his way, he grimaced and shook his head.

"Yeah, well Belhaven is the perfect place to hide. No woman with any sense at all would think to look there." She tried to wing him with her elbow, but caught thin air.

With a curt laugh, he rolled off the log and landed on his back. The sand still held a touch of warmth though the sun had begun to set over the sound side of the island. He flailed his legs so his feet kicked at the sky. Shoreward of the breakers, water receded to hush the scene.

Jaima fell back and soon raked the sky with him, her feet bare and free. "Scuttle like a crab when the fishermen are on the rampage." This time, when she winged him with her elbow, it landed a connection that lingered.

A coward, he defaulted to what he knew best. "Man, I wish those bluefish would run the inlet sooner than later."

"You and me both. I ask God for them every day."

Comforted that someone else talked to God about fish, he relaxed a little and let the sand massage his shoulder blades as he reached for her hand. They stayed clasped together like that until the sunlight grew dim, the waves ever breaking and washing back to sea.

Chapter 3

Harbor Days unfolded on the second Saturday of October which made the population of Manteo swell to intolerable. Jaima unpacked the last critter tub from the aquarium's van and headed back to their booth. Tucked between two wax myrtle bushes, that location helped dampen the hubbub of the crowd and isolate their educational exhibit. Director Fran Michaels preferred to head the outreach exhibit to remain connected to their admiring public. With a spot on the county commission opening next year, Fran had ulterior motives for keeping up appearances.

A vendor selling huge bags of kettle corn passed her on the approach route, leaving a salty-sweet scent in his wake. She might have to make a detour in his direction when she could finagle a break. Today, she would staff the mobile touch tank and try to remember the five fun facts she'd memorized about each marine resident. By far, the starfish were her favorite, wandering around the acrylic enclosure with pressurized tube feet that ensured a suction grip. Given their distraction, maybe she wouldn't have to people-watch all day.

Closer to the water, a boat engine revved. A microphone blared the name of Agua Aid in bold commercialism. She hoped the ruckus of the crowd would build to drown out that trumped-up clatter. She'd soon contribute while asking children questions to stimulate thoughts about marine organisms and their habitats.

"Good, you're back." Fran slipped an arm into a crisply ironed lab coat embroidered with the aquarium's logo. "I just spotted Mayor Priestly over at Full Sails Marina. Let me go touch base with him so he remembers to renew his membership."

"Sure, go ahead. I've got this." Not by accident, monetary solicitations fell outside of her job description. She smiled as she dumped several robust urchins into the touch tank. Thinking to gauge the temperature, she stuck several fingers into the trough and swirled the water. Two urchins adjusted their orientation in response.

A tall passer-by cast a shadow over the educational display. "Are you open for inquisitive early-birds—or should we come back later?"

When she looked up, she recognized the luckless fisherman from Belhaven accompanied by two boys of stair-step height. Before she could reply, a sea squirt attached to a synthetic piling made a discharge that shot like a fount above the water's surface.

The younger boy waved a small notebook at the sea squirt. "Did he just go to the bathroom?"

She crouched, treasuring the attentive look on the boy's face. "No, Gavin. Let's say he just breathed out, but using water, not air. That's part of his food filtering system."

Perry chuckled when the boy began to sketch the touch tank occupants. "I've seen some of those on dock pilings down at Wrights Creek Boating Access. They're closer to the sound where the water is still somewhat salty. I think Pantego Creek is too fresh for their liking."

"Probably," she replied with a tiny wink. "Okay, boys. Watch this." She tipped up one corner of the tank and exposed several sea squirts above the surface. In rapid sequence, each one fired off a stream of water and closed its top opening. "See? When exposed to air like at low tide, they close up and won't feed. They don't like being exposed between the tides, but they've learned to *tolerate* the exposure so they can inhabit an available niche in the ecosystem."

"That's like me eating broccoli," the older boy admitted with a snaggletooth smile. "I only tolerate it, because Mom works hard for our grocery money so I can't be wasteful."

Jaima produced a sticker bearing the aquarium's logo and offered it to him. "You should be rewarded for your no-waste attitude, Garrett." Without a word, the artist produced the cover of his sketch pad so she peeled the backing from another sticker and affixed it to the book. "Does anyone want to touch a wandering starfish?"

"I do," both boys replied in unison.

Perry leaned closer. "You're spoiling us, you know."

She gestured to the far end of the tank. "Perk of the job, I suppose. If you're passing by the popcorn man on your rounds, feel free to spoil me in return." When he looked surprised, she pulled several ones from her jeans pocket and waved the money at him. "I'm dead serious. That could easily represent my supper tonight."

He took and pocketed the wad, his eyes shimmering with masculine attention. "If I bring in a big haul later this month, I promise to take you out to dinner."

"Okay, Belhaven. You've got yourself a deal." She reached past the tank and shook his hand, immediately gaining a magnetic charge at the connection.

"Hey, this guy is about to escape." Garrett pointed to the largest starfish clasping the top of the container with three of its five arms.

She broke contact with the handsome fisherman to address the escapee. "You would think he'd know better than to leave this safe aqueous environment and land on dry ground."

"Maybe he feels compelled to cross Pamlico Sound," Perry suggested in a honey-soft voice. He waggled his eyebrows as if to add allure.

She held out a small glass rectangle used for featuring specimen and allowed the starfish to gain access. As she poised it over the boys' heads, she gave them a good look at the creature's underside.

"Man, look at all those suction tubes," Garrett said.

"More accurately called tube-feet," she replied. "That's how a starfish stays mobile."

Within seconds, Gavin flashed a picture of the animal. While the top looked realistic, he'd amplified the tube-feet to look monstrous. "Takeover of the starfish kingdom. That could really happen—which would be great!"

Perry gathered both boys to his side. "Okay, I'm seeing signs of too much TV watching. We'd better keep moving and see what else we can find. Dalton will need replacing at our booth after an hour, so my touring time is limited."

Gavin tugged at his shirttail. "Remember I want to see the boats."

He held out his palm until the boy slapped it. "Looks like the marina is calling us next."

"The age-old lure of the sea," she teased, putting the starfish back into the tank. "Now you know where to find me. After boat ogling, I hope you can discover the popcorn man."

"I look at the boat salesman like this." He held up his hands for blinders. "As for the popcorn man, now there's a place I can afford to pay attention. See you later this afternoon, Ms. Del-doll. Until then, don't lose any of your marine sidekicks." He left her with a half-cocked smile that popped a dimple onto one cheek.

She watched them cross the street heading for the marina. In less than a minute, Fran swept back into the confines of the exhibit. "My, that was a well-placed happenstance. Mayor Priestly plans to double his donation before year's end."

As the red plaid shirt that Perry sported faded into the crowd, she thought much the same thing. At further consideration, perhaps chance meetings weren't random happenstance. No man had ever crashed his boat in the surf right where she stood before Perry Manning ran aground. Whether that would ultimately double her gain still remained to be seen. In the meantime, she had a tank full of fascinating marine invertebrates to peddle.

~

No question he should ask Jaima out on a date, or they would never get any time alone. The possibilities haunted Perry all the way back to the aquarium's booth. *How can I afford to court a woman?* All his money kept the fishing business afloat. At least Dalton had booked four more tours in the next three weeks. Maybe he'd buy the fiberglass he needed for the stern repair on his boat after the first tour paid off.

He approached the aquarium booth, the bait dangling from his left hand. A broad-faced woman met him over the educational display. "Hey, is Jaima Delarie still around? She asked me to pick up this popcorn for her. Hope I'm not too late."

"No, she'll be back. I'm the aquarium's director, Fran Michaels."

"Perry Manning, ma'am. My brother and I run a fish tour business out of Belhaven."

Her expression gained interest. "Oh? We might need to hire out for fresh bait fish this winter to feed our tank occupants. Our volunteers are typically fair-weather fishermen."

He pulled a business card from his pocket. "We fish year-round. Give us a shout if you need fresh bait fish. I can pull a seine net for the smaller stuff. They get tricky off a hook."

Jaima shouldered past a wax myrtle bush. "Hey, Perry. Did you meet our director?"

He offered the business card across the display table. "Yes. We might be able to supply the aquarium some bait fish this winter."

Fran hefted two containers into her arms. "Sounds like a win-win arrangement to me. It's my turn to take the next load. Be right back."

He held his peace until the director disappeared toward the parking lot. "First, here's your popcorn. You forgot to tell me a preferred flavor, so I went with kettle corn."

"Great." She reached to take possession. "The caramel corn is too sweet for me. How'd you end up doing at your booth?"

He offered up the treat, but kept his grip around the plastic bag's ponytail. "Good enough to think about sharing a shrimp platter at a place I know down by Swan Quarter. What—"

"Wait a sec," she cautioned, a line creasing her brow.

A hunched figure shuffled into the booth space between them. "Time to hit cape pointe, Del-doll. The blues are running."

She clapped her hands together. "Praise God above. At long last, the bluefish have arrived. Sorry, Perry. I've got to bolt out of here. Monte, can you give me a lift by my place? I need to pick up my rods."

A tiny shock at being left behind rippled up his back, forcing a rash decision. "Hey, can I throw in with you guys? Dalton is taking the boys out for burgers."

Monte gave him a begrudging look. "Sure, the pointe is plenty wide. Keep the run hush-hush though, or every jack with a fishing pole will show up. I plan to get the jump on them."

Jaima packed a handful of urchins into a tub. "I need to tell Fran that I'm leaving."

The director appeared from the rear. "Tell me what?"

Jaima handed over the urchins. "Can you call in a volunteer to help you unpack at the aquarium? I need to hit cape pointe ASAP. The bluefish are throwing themselves onto shore."

Fran took the tub. "Of course. I know you live for that kind of thrill, so go for it."

Monte headed left toward a parking area with Jaima trailing right behind.

Perry pulled into their wake and bumped shoulders with her. "Listen, I need to borrow a rod. We drove up in Dalton's car which doesn't even have a trunk."

"I have seven surf rods but can only fish with two at a time," she replied in a breathless rush. "Take your pick from the rest. All are rigged for bottom fishing, but you can change out to lures if you'd prefer."

He began to catch a bit of the excitement as his blood pressure elevated. "No, let's see if they'll strike a hook. How's your bait supply?"

She stepped closer as if enjoying the collusion. "Ample—but frozen. I've been waiting for this run longer than I care to admit." The sideways look she gave him spoke volumes.

The ride over to her apartment transpired lightning-quick. They jumped out and dashed for the building. Monte left rubber on the pavement to head over the dunes.

Perry loaded rods into her SUV, excited for the pair-up.

Jaima returned at a brisk run after retrieving the bait bags from inside. "Cape pointe, here we come."

"I loaded two of the biggest coolers. Is that enough?"

She halted in her tracks. "Maybe for me. Are you planning to catch any fish?"

He collapsed on the storage shed with a chuckle, grabbed an old clunker of a cooler, and hoisted it into the car. "All set."

The drive down to Hatteras filled with the electrical charge of amped anticipation. They exchanged few words as the ice-encrusted shrimp bag rode the dashboard above the heating vent. The miles peeled off in a blur of sand dunes and pavement.

"Remember to keep two rigs in the water at all times. If you don't have a fish on, help me drag my catch out of the shore break. That's where most throw off the hook—or break the line."

"Fine. You do the same for me. We'll fish side by side. You pick the spot."

A pleasurable hum filled the front seat. "Maybe you're not as off-kilter as I once held."

Not to be downplayed, he had to protect his masculine pride. "You are mindful that I fish for a living—right?"

"Keep up if you can, Mr. Boat-in-dry-dock." She jerked the car off the pavement south of the lighthouse onto an obscure crossover, headed for the crest of the dune ridge.

"I suggest that you wear me like a shadow, Del-doll. After we slay these fish, then you can pass judgment on my ability to navigate the fickle waters of angling." He picked up the bait bag and snapped the ice chunk in half.

"Challenge duly accepted—which may be my final words spoken today. I don't like to chat much when I fish. Talking can be…distracting."

He held up his hands. "All fish, no talk. We'll compare notes after the melee." He glanced down the beach to find Monte knee-deep to the ocean in hip-waders. Again, the run had caught him short of being properly outfitted. One look at Jaima told him he'd find a way to make it work. He broke off several shrimp from the edge and worked to thaw the rest on his palms.

Jaima jammed the car to a halt and reversed to angle the rear bumper toward the breakers. In a heartbeat, she jumped from her seat and threw open the rear hatch. She loaded two lengthy surf rods in her hands, took possession of the shrimp, and hastened toward the shore.

He took a fleeting assessment of the old rods remaining and selected two with sturdy eyelets and taut monofilament lines. Thinking ahead, he added two rod holders for their spare poles. On the way to the beachfront, he took inventory of the rigs dangling off the terminal eyelet and found everything to be shipshape. Even with today's heightened wave activity, those lead weights should hold enough tension to keep the line tantalizing.

With a whiz of the reel, Jaima entered the battle. Mere seconds after the bale clicked into lock position, the tip of her rod bent nearly double. "Perry? Get down here!"

"Now shadowing you," he replied in a husky tone. "Let me get a line out first. Then I'll watch for your fish in the shallows." With a grunt, he shoved the rod holders deep into the sand. Fingering a shrimp loose from the pack, he pierced it across the hook, tripped the bale and timed his cast with a retreating wave. It sailed and entered the ocean south of her thrashing line.

"There," she said, backing up the slope. "Kick it if you have to, but do *not* lose my fish."

Energized by the challenge, he winked as he waded out. "That scenario doesn't happen in my world." In half a dozen steps, he had the leader line in his grip, a real beauty dangling off the business end. The silver-blue color down the fish's muscular flank mesmerized him for a second.

Jaima rushed to him and took possession. Dragging the fish toward the cooler, she nodded toward his rod. "Reel in yours, and I'll spot you at the waterline for payback."

"No—go ahead and get both your rods alternating. I'll do the same. We'll bring them in hand over fist until the run plays out. Let them lay on the beach to save time. See you on the backside." He lifted his rod and set the hook with authority. This first fish didn't disappoint, almost four feet long. With the leader straining, he cuffed the fish by the gill slits and dragged it onto shore in a heft of adrenaline.

For three-quarters of an hour, they alternated catching the next fish. He helped clear Jaima's line whenever possible, and she stopped to do the same for him in unspoken rhythm. Twice he took time to load the coolers. Several more fishing buggies assaulted cape pointe, driving down where Monte fished. Thankful for the private spot, their adventure turned cozy with sated satisfaction—and a glut of fish.

At the two-hour mark, sporadic hits stretched to nonexistent strikes. Jaima made a long cast, watched the sinker plunk into the ocean, and backed up toward her rod holder. She dug her bare feet into the sand, her stride stretched for balance, but her gaze perpetually on the ocean. "Maybe check your bait, Perry."

Lured by the liquid tone of her voice, he settled his rod into the holder instead. The bluefish run had likely ended, though they might hook a straggler with extended luck. After fitting the lid onto the closest cooler, he approached her in magnetic attraction. "Pretty incredible way to end a long Saturday, Del-doll. Thanks for having me along."

She broke her far-off gaze to regard him. "Listen, Perry. About that shrimp dinner you mentioned."

He placed a hand on her rod, unhooking the line where it rested taut on her finger. "May I?" When she released it to his care, he stooped and shoved it into the rod holder. Playing his next move on instinct, he'd let the lady object if she wanted. He stood close enough his toes touched hers in the sand. "No need to rush things, especially if you're not interested."

She lifted one hand and fingered a pocket on his

flannel shirt. "Or you could say there's no need to buy seafood—when you can catch it. I'm highly interested in that proposition."

While the meaning of her words tumbled around in his mind, he sensed her approach on tiptoe and became overtaken with a seizure of good sense. With his pulse pounding in his ears, he fit his arm around her back and drew her closer. Long wisps of silky hair almost concealed her blue eyes until a sea breeze blew at the last second to reveal an interested woman. The timing of a set hook flashed to mind about the time his lips brushed hers. All other sensation carried the heft of cresting tide from there, a sumptuous embrace which lasted several drumming waves.

"Hey," Monte called from his Suburban. "How'd you young-uns do down here?"

Jaima pulled away from his grasp, her pivot grinding sand across the top of his feet. "Uh, better than I expected. We didn't lose one fish. Got 'em on and kept 'em on."

"That's the best report an old salty can give," he replied with a nod. "I gotta go home and start cleaning fish, or I'll be up past midnight."

She waved as he departed and then let the hand fall on her hip. "Oh, wow. I never gave one thought as to cleaning all these fish at my apartment. We caught too many to take inside."

"How about my place? We have a fillet table rigged with running water out on the dock." He stood stock still, braced for rejection.

"That's a sulphur-stinking blood-and-guts offer to spend more time together if I've ever heard one."

A slight curl of her lips followed. "You need a ride home, anyway."

"We'll cut fillets and steaks, then ice down the coolers so you can bring the fish home."

She pulled the rod out of the holder and began to reel in the line. "Let's stop for ice along Whalebone Junction. You, know, I'm thinking Sea Foam might be in for a banquet tonight."

"Not just the cat. I'm planning to throw the first fish I caught lengthwise across my fire pit and slow cook it over hot coals. That will be our dinner."

Her bottom rig dribbled up the sandy slope, lacking any bait. "Toss in a baked potato on the side, and you've got a date."

He packed up the fish camp until the last rod had been stowed. Taking one cooler handle in his grasp, he waited for her to assume the other end. When her gaze snagged his, the gravity hit him full force. "Thanks for making this day memorable. I don't think I could ever forget it."

She pushed a wink at him. "Got 'em on, kept 'em on."

He groaned with the lift. Today, success bore a substantial weight. A gritty slide secured part of the catch in her hatch. A twin cooler soon rested beside the first. The third cooler proved problematic. "Okay, what should we do now?"

She headed for the door. "If I lower the back seats, it levels to extend the storage capacity." After a few tugs, the seat backs fell into compliance.

He shoved the twin coolers until gaining the needed width. Up front, two empty seats remained side by side. *Now set the hook.* A bolder link-up, he planned to hold her hand all the way to Belhaven.

Chapter 4

A crisscrossed cord sectioned off the cape pointe beachfront into something of a chess board, with ghost crabs for pawns. Jaima tried not to single out the imprint of her own tires from only days ago. Already finished with the upper transect, she saw clear evidence the larger crabs had sought shelter up here in the dunes. Unwilling to jump to conclusions, she needed to accomplish two more hours of data collecting.

With the rising tide about to peak, she pocketed her logbook and ambled toward the shore. Her idle thoughts about fishing later took a wander in the direction of a handsome, hazel-eyed fisherman who had cooked her dinner Saturday night, cleaned her bluefish, and asked permission to see her again. October always ended trick-or-treat style, but she wasn't in any mood for pranks. A steady job and a roof over her head sufficed for now. *Or does it?*

A wave pushed the flotsam higher onto shore where a piece of plastic trash caught her attention. Before she could stoop to collect it, her phone rang. The aquarium number appeared on her screen. "Jaima here. Can I help you?"

In response, a low growl traveled up the line. "It's a dark day for us, Jaima." A controlled sob cut the speaker short.

Prickles ran up Jaima's arm. The aquarium director bore many flaws, but the woman typically abstained from all-out melodrama. "Go ahead and tell me what you're dealing with, Fran. Together, we can handle it."

"While opening the displays, at the circular touch tank I found the occupants belly-up. Lord help me, it's just horrendous in here."

"Oh, wow. What's the program schedule like this morning?" She dug her heels into the sand to keep from wavering in the sea breeze.

"The elementary school from Sandpiper comes in at ten o'clock for a full circuit of interpretive programs and a movie prior to taking lunch on the grounds. Guess I'll have to rope off the touch tank. There's no way I want them to see this disaster."

Jaima fumed at what could have happened over the weekend to taint the tank. "Listen. Get some help to pull out all the expired stingrays. Drain all the water and refill the tank. Replace the rays with some juvenile horseshoe crabs I have back in the wet lab. Hey, those resident touch tank invertebrates are tough. Do any of them seem alive?"

"Well, yes, the starfish are moving slow, and the sea squirts are closed shut. Ugh. The biggest starfish has extruded his stomach."

"There—he's trying to tell you something. If we had an escape ladder, he would have pulled out to safety. We'll have to give that some consideration.

Leave some water with the dead rays in a tub. When I return, I'll run a sample and try to get to the bottom of this."

"Oh, dear. I think I just heard school buses pull into the lot. Gotta get busy playing undertaker for an innocent flock of stingrays. Bye."

Jaima buried her phone in a back pocket and let the imagery of a flock of flying rays distract her for a moment. Out along the horizon, a powder blue boat hummed by on its way to a blissful day of offshore fishing. Ill fate kept her landlocked today. She approached the roped-off grid, determined to finish her task. The mass die-off back at the aquarium needled her level sensibilities. Perhaps a staff member had been careless, though the automatic water filtration system always ran without a hitch.

The instant her rationale headed toward the possibility of intentional harm, a beast-sized ghost crab showed itself at the opening of the nearest burrow. "Consider yourself measured, Hercules," she said with conviction. After finding her place in the logbook, she recorded the local population until she'd exhausted every grid square. *Chess or dodge ball?* Unsure what game might be unraveling, she headed for the parking lot to reconnect with humankind.

~

Perry caught the football in the crook of his arm, the added heft symbolizing his nephew's increased strength. "Pretty good rotation on that one, Garrett. I think it had touchdown potential, for sure."

The boy grinned. "Dad says I can try out for

flag football this year. Tryouts start the first of November for city league."

The local recreation department strived to emphasize sportsmanship over scores which kept the teams even and prevented the competition from becoming mean-spirited. Two years ago, Manning Fishing had sponsored Garrett's basketball team. If finances didn't improve, that sponsorship wouldn't happen again, much to his chagrin. "Okay, remember what I told you. Keep your weight up on the balls of your feet to stay quick and agile."

Dalton emerged from the front door of his house and glanced up the street. With a jerk, he circled his mouth with one hand. "Caw-caw, caw-caw."

Perry recognized their secret emergency call and tossed the ball back to Garrett. As he shooed Gavin onto the steps, a familiar car floated down his driveway. "Tell Beth I won't make it for dinner tonight, after all."

Dalton guided both boys through the doorway. "I'll tell her, bro. Whatever spawned this meet-up, try to make it count."

He trailed a thumbs-up in response and hastened to his own yard where the unexpected—a drop-in visit—might be transpiring. He quelled the excitement building in his chest by taking a short breath. Never one to presume too much, at least she'd found Belhaven again.

Jaima swung her legs from the car and stood. When her loose hair cleared her face, a red tempest rimmed her sea-blue eyes. "Hey there."

Her emotional struggle struck his midsection like a right-handed jab. "Hey yourself. What gives?"

"Tragedy at the aquarium today. I need a boat. Can you get me out on the sound?"

He turned both palms skyward. "Sure, anything you need. Lend me three seconds to let Dalton know we need to use his boat." He backpedaled toward Aunt Sally's house. "It's good to see you—tragedy notwithstanding." He jogged and shouted a quick message to Dalton through the screen door. By the time he returned, she'd opened the rear hatch on her car.

"We have company—the victims of the tragedy."

"Fine. I'll carry the tub to the dock. You fill me in on what's happened—if you can." He scooped up the plastic tub that looked like a super-sized version of the ones she'd used at Harbor Days for the display invertebrates.

"Fran made her rounds like usual this morning, opening up the exhibit halls. When she came to the touch tank, she found all the stingrays belly-up and stacked against the flow filter. Just like that, they're fine one minute and then dead the next."

He waited for the path to narrow so they could walk closer. "How does that make any sense? Nature doesn't work that way. Did somebody make a slip-up?"

She shook her head. Seconds later, she caught a sob in her fist. A fresh tear soon rolled down her cheek. "No, turns out, it was an intentional act to harm."

His footfall drummed the dock as he crossed to Dalton's boat. The unfairness of the loss tightened the skin at the base of his neck. Hoisting the tub onto the rear bench, he motioned for her next.

She stepped toward him, but avoided eye contact. "I just wanted…" She grasped for his hand and clung to it. "I just wanted to give them a burial at sea. They deserve to go back."

He wrapped her in one arm and guided her into the vessel. "Pamlico Sound, here we come. No further explanation needed." He cleared the stern line and fired up the twin engines.

She sniffled and sat across from the captain's seat. "Breakneck?"

He eased a smile into one cheek. "That's the only throttle position Dalton knows. As you're aware with fishing, sometimes it matters who gets there first. Still, it does seem like bragging to name the boat after his lust for speed." Though she turned away to stare at the creek bank, he thought he saw the corner of her eyes crinkle in response to his jest.

A quiet ten-minute trip out to open water transpired with only engine hum to keep his mindset on even keel. The week's end would close out the peaceable month of October, and then November would hit like the proverbial wrecking ball. He hated when the fringing marsh grass died, as it seemed to evoke an end to the regenerative power of coastal living. Somehow, he resisted such a blunt cessation.

Jaima laid a cool hand across his arm. "This is far enough."

He eased the throttle and the bow dropped to present the sound waters as an unbroken horizon. "Tell me how you want to handle the animals."

She stooped beside the tub and opened its lid. "Help me touch each one and bid them a fond goodbye. Then we can release them over the stern."

He accepted a small specimen with a brown back and lighter-colored belly. It bore the texture of fine-grit sandpaper. "Wow, their skin is rougher than I thought, not smooth."

She glanced up fighting another round of tears. "Yes, much to the delight of school children in our five-county area. In God's wonderful design, he gives us much to admire." She picked up a larger ray and stroked its back. "Goodbye, sport. You tolerated some unrelenting hands-on learning, but ultimately couldn't stand the lethal pH fluctuation. Thank you for your service to Roanoke Aquarium."

He mimicked her release, placing them face-to-face over the gunwale at the sound's edge. "Why make pH the bad guy in this die-off?" His incredulous tone held a husky croak.

Her eyes closed as if to blot out the ugly truth. "The tank water tested with high levels of hydrochloric acid. The pH shift prevented proper respiration and eventually ruptured cell walls. I'm not sure of the exact necropsy, except to say it was total systems failure at that level."

When a tear rolled down her cheek, he quelled his first impulse to choke the perpetrator. Instead, he leaned toward her and kissed the corner of her eye. "Thanks for sharing your heroes with me." He removed two more stiffened bodies from the tank and nudged her to take one. "Here's to those who dedicate themselves to teaching about the wonders of the sea—one gentle touch at a time."

She rubbed a knuckle against the spot he'd kissed and lowered her animal into the water. "Somehow, I knew you would understand."

Over two dozen animals later, the ritual had run its full course. Perry dropped into the rear bench, closed the empty tub, and then stared out over the water. "It's all coming to an end in November, an ugly brown-rimmed end of season where nothing can grow."

She pulled the tub in the hull and sat beside him, leaning her head onto his shoulder. "Don't say nothing can grow. Remember the water stays warm for longer, so the fish live on."

The heat of fresh tears soon soaked through his hoodie, making him more determined to keep something alive. When her lips wandered up past his jawline to meet his, he found the tender grace to celebrate being among the land of the living. *Hold on.* He would if only he could.

Chapter 5

Perry sat behind the wheel of his truck while his kid brother jogged up to the information board. Posting flyers at Wrights Creek Boat Landing seemed fruitless at first mention, but Dalton had insisted they cover every possible contact. Several men stood around the loading dock as a citified SUV backed toward the water line to set a sleek ski boat loose. The sound had plenty of room for casual recreation, as long as it didn't prevent him from earning a living.

Preoccupied by contemplations of picking up another line of work for the winter months, he lost track of time. When he glanced up again, two dark-haired men exchanged comments with Dalton, loaded with lots of negative body language. Before his brother broke from the group, the shortest guy shoved his shoulders as if expelling him from the water's edge.

Dalton crossed the lot and got back in the cab with a sheepish look on his face. "Well, I posted the flyer. If that bunch will leave it alone, we might gain a job or two from the ad."

"What did those guys want?"

"Nothing. They asked around for any information about the guy who ran his boat aground on Cape Hatteras the first of the month. Seems like he may have forgotten to deliver something they owned." He straightened and glanced across the cab. "Does that mumbo-jumbo mean anything to you?"

"No, not a thing. You didn't let on it was me, did you?"

"Nope. I claimed I didn't know about the shipwreck. Truth be told, if you're moonlighting by delivering contraband on the side, I really don't know anything about it."

He locked both hands onto the steering wheel. "If I was peddling something illegal, you don't think I'd be living hand-to-mouth like this, do you, Dalton? I fish for a living. That's all there is. Those guys are searching for somebody else."

Dalton nodded. "*We* fish for a living, brother. Since we're partners, we'd better not have any secrets held between us."

He wheeled the truck around and headed for the exit. "Let's take the boat out on the sound and wet a few hooks. The manager at Value Market always buys anything we catch."

Dalton popped on his favorite fishing hat. "That suits me fine."

"Good. Now tell me. Why'd you let that guy shove you around like that?"

His brother whistled his exhalation. "Carlos used to play tackle for the team out of Little Washington. He tried to wring my neck more than once during conference play."

"You can't beat an old football rivalry. Still, a seasoned running back can throw down a pretty good block to gain an advantage when he has to."

"You've got that right. I just let him push me around, trying not to cast any suspicion your way. We don't need more trouble in our neck of the woods. We're already down one boat."

Once the road opened out, he pumped up his speed, thinking gas might be cheaper than burning daylight right now. A pair of tear-rimmed eyes flickered to mind, stirring a deeper reaction. "Just so you know there's been trouble over at the aquarium. Intentional trouble."

"Like what?"

"Somebody poisoned the touch tank with acid. Killed the whole batch of stingrays."

"Man, that's low. Hey, don't tell my boys. They loved that starfish."

"That little fella survived—just barely." Though he tried to hold back further comment, a growl rumbled up his throat to testify that the matter remained far from over.

"What about the aquarium lady? You gonna keep from telling me about her?"

"She's a soft spot for me. A definite soft spot."

Dalton turned back to him and watched out the window as they skimmed by a fringing marsh. "At least she loves to fish. Still, you're not highly sophisticated, brother. Maybe you should try to up your charm level and act more high-minded."

"Turns out, she finds academic types boring. Her real passion is the ocean. We have that in common. Anyway, I've already set the hook."

"And now you have to reel her in." A sly smile followed his assertion. "Ultimate Fish Finders—the guide, not the gadget."

As he turned down Back Sound Road, the how-to aspect of that courting task began to goad him. Dinner by candlelight might fan the flames, but how could he afford the bill? "I really need to catch a cooler-full of fish." For a brief second, his throat constricted until he realized Pamlico Sound never backed a man into a corner. No, he had plenty of space to live—if he could only muster some courage to walk on the tempestuous waters of courtship.

~

The doodled scribbles filling up Jaima's desk calendar bore proof that something weighed her thoughts. Yesterday's brief visit to haul off Edwina's garbage left her unsettled, as the old woman seemed sullen though she didn't divulge the reason. Even the freezer bag full of bluefish steaks she'd brought along hadn't lifted the octogenarian's spirits. Maybe she wasn't eating right, as her trash bag sure seemed light—or possibly she hadn't burned anything lately.

A knock on the office door proved a welcome intrusion. Fran peered inside as if testing the air before walking in. "Hey, what gives this morning? The fish are missing you."

"Sorry I've turned introvert this morning. I'll go by at lunch and baby talk the main tank occupants. Since you're here, stay and let me pick your brain a minute."

"Okay, a minute sounds about right to cover my

cranium front to back. What's up?"

"I have a friend who seems down lately. I really respect her a lot. Part of their family's colorful coastal heritage includes helping build the Wright Brothers Memorial."

"Aha. An old-timer then. Our senior citizens can get really down when they're isolated for too long. If I am elected to the County Commission, I plan to spearhead an effort to get Dare County a senior center with a fully-functional kitchen that can offer low-cost meals."

She propped both elbows on the desktop and held her head in her hands. "Don't let this sound crazy because so much time has gone by, but the government slighted her grandfather and never paid for all his labor to build the memorial. He worked a two-mule team pulling a sled to build the sand into a hill. Imagine how arduous that must have been."

"And what? You want to make it right?"

"Is that possible? I mean settle something out of court?"

"Yes, haven't you ever heard of making reparations? That's how the government offers an apology to a wronged entity to acknowledge a past injustice. Sometimes they pay money, and other times they make a token gesture instead, like naming a building after someone."

"It sounds like I need to address the possibility of requesting such reparations then. I think it might strike a positive note for this particular friend of mine."

"Good idea. Remember, you have representation in Raleigh. Contact your congressman for help and be frank about the matter. The Wright Brothers Memorial is a national treasure, and it brings Dare County strong tourist dollars, too. Play upon his sense of fairness."

She finger-combed her hair back into a ponytail and searched the drawer for a band. "Something tells me a little kindness out of the blue might be a balm for the weary."

"You're right about that. I've got to go tackle my quarterly report for the Board meeting next. November will be here before we know it."

"Perish the thought," she replied with a snap of her fingers. The star drawn on her calendar reminded her of a personal milestone that would transpire two days before October could end. Yet another birthday might come and go without any significance. For some inexplicable reason, a quiet dock on Pantego Creek popped to mind without solicitation—perhaps the only place on earth where time could afford to stand still.

∼

Three solid days of fiberglass work managed to mend the rift in the stern of his boat, a wave-pounding penalty for his idiot move beaching on cape pointe. Perry shimmied the towel over his right shoulder blade with a moan. A hot shower hadn't helped much. The fiberglass bond would set up and make his vessel seaworthy again, right in time for their next big gig—a two-boat fishing outing for reps of a new pharmaceutical company out of Charlotte. Though Dalton had bragged nonstop over landing that tour, it paid well enough to get him through the end of the year. If only the fish would bite, they might book again for a follow-up outing.

He stepped to the old bureau to find something cottony soft to stave off the evening's slight chill. Opting for a long-sleeved T-shirt and some old jeans, he made quick work of getting dressed. Once the shirt settled into place, his stomach growled in protest of skipping lunch. "Right. Next stop—the fridge." With any luck, he could find a fresh vegetable to go with his specialty side dish, concocted earlier in the week.

The moment he touched the refrigerator handle, the doorbell rang. Living in a family hub, such interruptions landed on his doorstep all the time. He pulled the front door open looking down to focus on Gavin or Garrett, but found the hem of a wispy open-weave sweater instead. When he glanced up, Jaima hid her face with a large bag marked with a seafood logo. "Wow, you delivery people get better looking all the time. I forget. Did I order something?"

She pulled the bag aside to show off a feminine pout. "No, I ordered something."

He reached for the bag but missed. "Well, then why the surprise visit?"

Her eyes flashed dark for the briefest instant. "Today's my birthday. I could either stay in Manteo where the event would go unheralded or strike out to find a better way to celebrate. For some reason, visions of your dock enticed me to make the drive out. Would you care to share a fried shrimp dinner-for-two?"

The slight tremble of her bottom lip after posing the question tugged at his heart. "I'm definitely blessed to take part in your birthday feast. We'll eat out on the dock to make it memorable. Let me bring along an appetizer—my infamous smoked fish dip. Once you try it, you'll be hooked." A tiny wink chased his braggart claim.

A blush worked up her neck to make her eyes almost luminous. "So unlike a fisherman to give any warning in advance."

He backpedaled toward the refrigerator. "Want some tea? I made a fresh pitcher last night."

"Sure. Bring it in a carafe or something. I have an old quilt in the back of my car to sit on, since I don't remember seeing a picnic table back there."

The comment resonated, but he tried to toss it off with a shake of his head. "Manning men tend to be all work and no play. I don't think anyone ever saw that old dock as more than a workstation." He grabbed the tub of dip and poured the tea in two travel cups. Ready to leave, he found her leaning against the door jamb so he brushed her arm while reaching for the light switch. After slipping into his deck shoes, he cocked his brow and locked gazes with his guest. "Let's go celebrate the birthday of someone special who managed to be born two thin days before Halloween."

"Yeah, the trick-or-treat prank fell on my mom that year, for sure." She stuffed the seafood bag into the crook of his arm and stepped out onto the carport. "I'll grab the quilt."

He flicked on the light that illuminated most of the backyard. "What number are we celebrating? And don't make me call your mother to find out the answer."

She bundled the quilt against her chest and laughed. "No need. I'm twenty-nine and holding—for the first time."

"That looks good against my thirty-one years of wisdom and maritime seasoning," he teased. "Speaking of which, I think you'll enjoy the Old Bay seasoning in my dip. I only make it with bluefish, so I owe this batch to you. Funny you should show up to claim the last helping."

She walked a half-step behind, nudging his arm with her shoulder. "I could have come out earlier if not for battling my pride. Most women would wait to be invited."

He froze in his tracks. "I'm too inept at this dating game to follow the rules. From now on, there's no pride issue between us. You have a standing invitation to come here. Now that my boat is fixed, I might even be able to afford to date you." He took off for the dock, fearful he'd admitted too much about his ridiculous state of impoverishment. Once the soles of his shoes struck wood planks, he waited for her to catch up.

A flounce of the heavy quilt set the stage for a shared meal. Jaima took the far side and sat cross-legged facing the creek. "Hand me some of our feast, and I'll set the food out."

He lowered the bag to her, but kept the drinks in the crook of his arm. "Maybe I should have brought my camping lantern out here."

"No, please. I like the duskiness. It feels rich. See? The water seems to gleam with aqua fading from the western sky."

Sounding like poetry with the airy lilt in her

voice, he began to sense the richness, too. He knelt, and then settled on the quilt near her to watch the creek shimmer with color. "Allow me to thank God for this bountiful setting and for takeout food I didn't have to cook. What a blessing." When her hand found his, he squeezed it tight. "Dear Maker of the Universe, we thank you for this creek, the inland sound it fills, and the vast ocean it fringes. Here we sit like two small boats that have, by some miracle, run together at the edge of your dock. We ask you to bless our friendship and make it count for something out of the ordinary. Especially bless Jaima tonight on her birthday. And thank you for this seafood. Amen."

She made a tiny noise in her throat, suggesting an inner wrangle. Her thumb caressed the top of his hand. "Perry, I want you to know that I think about you all the time." Her hushed admission trickled over the fringing marsh where something splashed in the shallows.

He picked up her hand and pressed it against his lips. "Good. At least I'm not going crazy by myself. But starvation is another matter, so let me win you over with my smoked fish dip." He raised the tub and removed the lid with his teeth. "Grab a corn chip and give it a try."

Without protest, she dug into the tub and took a mouthful. "Hmmm. So good."

He braced a cup of tea between her ankles. "Make a wish, birthday girl."

She scooped another chip through the dip. "Fine. I wish you would feed me my shrimp by hand, one at a time." She ate the chip and another musical hum followed.

He leaned closer to whisper his compliance. When his jawline scraped her cheek, he yielded to a tactile reaction that fed a different sort of hunger. Dusk fell until the sky twinkled with far-set stars while he alternated shrimp with kisses like manna stolen from the sea.

Chapter 6

Older students meant louder noise in the hallway. Determined to get her third quarter reports completed for two federal grants, Jaima rose to put a heavy wooden door between her and a steady disruption of concentration. One tug at the knob shut the portal—almost. The toe of a white rubber boot worn by local fishermen kept her from total success. When she peeked through the crack, she found Monte with a weighed look on his face. "Hey, you. What gives coming into the aquarium today? Wouldn't you rather be catching fish?"

"Well, I'll let the tide rise first. Thought you might want to know Edwina isn't doing well. When I stopped by this morning, she didn't want to get out of bed."

A foreboding swept prickles down her arm. "Uh-oh. That's not normal for Miss Spitfire."

Monte shook his head. "Wondered if you could stop by her place later…you know, to check on her. She always seems to get a lift from your visits."

She glanced through the office window to check the sky. "Okay, you have my word. If it's not pouring down rain, I'll duck by for a short visit.

Maybe she needs to see her doctor."

Monte glanced up through his graying brow. "I wouldn't suggest that option to her, at least not right off the bat. I'm guessing her ailment may be all up here." He tapped his temple with a bent finger. "I'm off to hunt down some bait fish."

"Try under the little bridge beside Full Sails Marina. The mosquito fish are usually thick through there, but you'll have to use a net."

Monte gave a generous wink. "Be careful not to tell all your secrets, Del-doll." With a sweeping bow, he disappeared from the doorway.

Instead of returning to her desk, she fidgeted around the office, straightening vertical files and neatening stacks of aquarium literature that needed to be re-filed in the media room. Brooding conjecture about Edwina's well-being darkened her mood as she decided to visit after work, rain or shine. She could do that much and try to brighten the old woman's day. Maybe the chill of November hadn't set well in her aging joints.

The squeak of an opening door trailed a soft knock. A man hid behind the door but his hazel eyes gave him away. "Ms. Delarie, would you have a moment for a passing visitor?"

She set her hands on her hips in mild protest. "First Monte and now you. Are Tuesdays that easy to disrupt?"

"Pretty easy." Perry shouldered into the room with a timid smile. "I thought I saw Monte leaving the parking lot. What gives with him?"

"He asked me to visit Edwina. She's down in the dumps over something and didn't want to get out of bed this morning. Guess I'll drop by after work and check on her." As she glanced out the door at the passing sixth-grade class, she spotted the director with a scowl of disapproval on her face. "Hey, let me show you my new wet lab down the hall."

He stepped out of the office and gestured for her to lead. "I really came to deliver a simple invitation, but I stand eager to learn like a schoolboy at your insistence."

Once they'd gained some privacy down the research wing, she allowed the rhythmic bumping of his shoulder to smooth a few ruffled feathers. "I'm really proud of this lab. We're working to make Big Pharma environmentally responsible. In collaboration with the university, I've developed a prototype nursery for raising horseshoe crabs. A resource consortium for the eastern seaboard wants to require pharmaceutical companies to regenerate horseshoe crab numbers before they decimate the entire Atlantic population."

He glanced up at the handwritten sign. "Limulus Lab. That sounds nurturing."

She smiled and flipped on the light switch. Juvenile horseshoe crabs shifted inside of troughs where seawater ran through open channels. "Here's the first batch of mitigation animals. We plan to make the drug companies replenish the ecosystem with these new upstarts."

"Why are they interested in these crabs?" He wiggled a finger in front of a hefty specimen and the creature seemed intrigued at the visual stimulation.

"Not only are hospitals using the blue blood of horseshoe crabs as an astringent to clean equipment, but drug companies also use LAL extracted from their blood to purify any injected drugs from bacteria. Limulus blood has the capability to clump around bacteria and thus sterilizes vaccines for human use."

"Do the critters survive the blood donation?"

"Common practice involves extracting one-third of the animal's blood, and then returning the crab to its native habitat. Many die along the route—an estimate hundred thousand a year. That's why we want compensation for their replacement. The crazy thing is, a lab-synthesized alternative exists, but for some unspecified reason drug companies are hesitant to switch over."

A guilty look swept his face as he ran a hand over his hair. "Dalton booked a two-boat fishing party with that new drug company out of Charlotte for this coming weekend. I hope they aren't involved with this Limulus blood-letting."

"Sure, they are. Almost every pharmaceutical company is involved with LNL to some extent. It guarantees effectiveness of their drug vaccines by sterilizing bacteria that could make people sick. Maybe your fishing outing represents a rare chance to show them how important habitat conservation is for native marine life."

He grinned and looked up at her. "Want to first mate for me and teach the lesson yourself? Uncle Glenn's boat is plenty big enough for a two-person crew."

Non-confrontational at heart, something about

that direct interface rubbed her the wrong way. "No, I'd better reserve my time for trash-collecting duties at Edwina's. They empty our apartment dumpster on Saturday mornings, and then I hide her trash inside along with mine."

"Here's a more genuine invitation then. We're giving Dalton's wife Beth a surprise birthday party at my house on Friday night. She turns the big three-oh, and Dalton couldn't let that happen without some kind of celebration. Can you join us for dinner and birthday cake?"

She flicked off the lights, sensing some finality in their visit. "At last, you make me an offer that doesn't smell like fish. Count on me to be there with pita chips and spinach dip. What time?" She slipped out of the lab and waited for him in the hall. Once he joined her, she led toward the aquarium's front entrance.

"Let's say seven o'clock. That gives Beth plenty of time to get home from work and suspect we might be up to something. Plus, you need time to drive over."

"Great. I'll make the dip ahead Thursday night. This sounds like fun."

"Manning-style fun anyway." He knocked a knuckle across her chin at the front door. "See you Friday. Until then, I'll keep my eye out for wayward horseshoe crabs. In fact, I'm headed down to Hatteras bight from here."

She hung on his gaze for a gratifying moment. "Tell Monte I said Operation Sunshine is underway at Edwina's."

He leaned a bit closer. "I'll take a little of that

sunny treatment...say late Friday night."

She shooed him out of the door with a flick of her wrist. *Sunshine and nighttime don't mix.* Handsome as distractions went, Perry still hadn't helped her write those quarterly reports. Or had he?

~

A hush fell over Perry's front room as anticipation reached critical levels. Uncle Glenn had corralled Garrett and Gavin in his long arms while Aunt Peggy stooped to whisper some encouragement to quiet them. Nearby, a rectangular sheet cake had gained a triangular wedge to resemble a boat with foamy waves crashing over the bow.

Dalton dimmed the dining room light and then crouched behind a recliner.

The sweet scent of peppermint added a tickle to the moment. Jaima's hand brushed his shoulder. "What comes to mind when the lights grow dim?"

"I'm thinking what a rich man I am." He bent and kissed her hand.

She hummed and handed him his party mask, courtesy of the aquarium. She placed the starfish over her face and knelt behind the bar.

By all appearances, tonight he played the role of a puffer fish. At least its boxy profile covered most of his face. Maybe he could flirt with the starfish and not gain a penalty. He knelt beside her, tipped the puffer to one side, and delivered a wink at the collusion. The chain on the screen door jingled the slightest bit. Then the side door pushed open.

Beth stepped inside. "Yoo-hoo. Perry? I brought you the leftover Halloween candy like Dalton asked. Is anybody home?"

Dalton popped up first and flicked on the light switch. "Happy birthday, Beth!"

Aunt Peggy orchestrated a round of the birthday song while the boys jumped up and down in glee.

Beth stood there, mouth open and eyes wide with disbelief. "How on earth did I not find out you were planning this?"

Gavin ran to her and wrapped her legs in a hug. "We got hush money, Mom. We couldn't tell you. I promised Uncle Perry I wouldn't blab."

He raised his arms to declare innocence. "Happy birthday, Sis. Welcome to the thirties decade where life is better than fine."

Beth held up a halting palm. "Wait—no aging jokes tonight. I'm still adjusting." She dropped the bag of candy in Dalton's hands to receive a hug from Aunt Peggy.

While he delayed in the kitchen, Jaima swept around him and waited her turn to greet the guest of honor. To his delight, she gave Beth a full hug and exchanged a girlish giggle. A timer dinged so he took the chicken wings out of the oven and added them to the buffet. "Okay, folks. Dinner is ready. Uncle Glenn, would you do the honors and say grace for us?"

As a rhythmic prayer followed, Perry could hear a hint of his father's voice in Glenn's tone, a family resemblance that felt more like a blessing on this particular occasion. Before the benediction, a gentle nudge let him know he enjoyed feminine companionship tonight, a welcomed addition to the passage of time. When her fingertips touched his, he balled his hand around hers to hold on tight.

"Woot-woot," Dalton exclaimed. "We're having chicken wings tonight. I hope you picked up some hot sauce, too."

"Peggy wouldn't let me get it too hot," Uncle Glenn confessed. "Still, the Asian wings have a spicy kick."

"I like spicy," Garrett replied with a grin.

Peggy stooped to place a kiss on the boy's head. "That's because you're just like your daddy, little man. Someday, you'll be the fisherman borrowing Uncle Glenn's boat. Perry, you've forgotten the napkins."

He snapped his fingers and headed for the pantry, gliding on a cloud of happiness because his family had gathered to spend the evening together—his favorite pastime. Before he could open the pantry door, Jaima had beaten him to the retrieval.

"Let me make myself at home and help you." She located the napkins and took out a handful while Gavin squealed with delight upon spying the boat-cake.

He rested his chin on her shoulder for a private moment behind the pantry door. The soft wool of her sweater felt like a caress. "I think I'm falling in love with you, Del-doll. Want to tell me what to do with that?"

Her eyes sparkled like the ocean at noon. "I'd hold tight to that sentiment, Mr. Fisherman."

"Got 'em on, keep 'em on."

"Perry?" Aunt Peggy called. "Where are those napkins?"

Jaima winked and stepped from the pantry, flailing the napkins in plain sight.

Perry followed to find the family members swarming on the buffet like a pod of killer whales encircling a school of fish. *My precious interfering family.* When Jaima stuffed a spinach-dipped chip into his mouth, he took it like a penalty—remarkable flavor aside. In a deft move, he stole the tongs from Dalton and maneuvered a stack of crispy wings onto his empty plate. From there, the party buoyed him through the festive night like an unclaimed mooring float waiting for its ship to come in.

Chapter 7

November puffed a cheek-stinging breeze across the Outer Banks which left Manteo little protection. Jaima strode toward the post office with the outgoing aquarium newsletter, only a week late getting mailed. Her Limulus Lab feature filled the entire second page, where she wore her best smile and a lab coat to look more professional. Today, the wind tore at the flaps in her cargo pants, a hint that blustery fieldwork would claim the rest of her day.

The gruff clerk in the bulk mailing facility made quick work of logging in the banded parcel pieces, so she returned to the parking lot in record time. If the day could gain ten degrees, her comfort out on the study transect at Hatteras pointe would be much improved. Ghost crabs didn't like cool weather, so they'd stay deep in the burrow sulking until the sun passed overhead.

She spotted a thick plume of smoke only seconds before a siren pierced the salt-laden air.

Close by, curiosity overrode her senses so she let the smoke lure her like a beckoning signal. She crossed the street to Full Sails Marina as three men ran past her toward the docks. Several boats slid from their berths and made for open water. On the second dock from the rear, a vessel sat tethered to the iron cleats, its cuddy cab engulfed in flames.

Fire trucks screamed onto the scene, rolling down a service entrance flanking the marina. Crew members soon shouted instructions as heavy hoses unreeled in an attempt to reach the fire-stricken boat. The scene swarmed with frantic effort, making her feel dizzy. She grabbed a braided cordon rope fencing off the front dock and watched as the men try to work a miracle. In full rebellion, a ball of fire rolled toward the boat's stern and spread the inferno.

Time crept to slow-motion as firemen toiled to get a stream of water onto the flames. A second hose filled with foamy retardant seemed to squelch the fire, shortening its height until soon only smoke and buckled decking remained. The bow of the boat lacked scorching, where she noticed the powder-blue color for the first time. Familiar recall haunted her immediately, as she'd seen that boat go out to sea almost daily since early summer. *Poor fisherman.* He would be out of work this winter and no doubt down on his luck from the loss, too.

A police car rushed onto the scene next. Its black-clad officers intercepted the two brothers who owned the marina. A heated conversation transpired. Another man dressed in business clothes began taking pictures in a panoramic sweep.

The urge to flee struck her full-force, but she couldn't evade the man's camera. When it clicked in her direction, she felt somehow trapped inside the marina's misfortune. Without conscious effort, her feet broke into a trot across the street to regain the safety of her SUV. Today, the little island where she lived tilted out of kilter, though science wouldn't interpolate such change. A chill ran up her spine as she started the car and put it through its paces to flee the tragic scene for cape pointe—her ever-waiting refuge from the tainted haunts of humankind.

~

Perry stepped further into the workshop's bay, grateful for shelter out of the brisk wind. The hull restoration work continued on his shipwrecked boat, and today he would extend the new fiberglass surface all the way under the boat's hull to the center keel. Then, he could pretend the boat possessed half a fix—until he could repeat the same patch for the opposing side.

The hoist he'd rigged held tension to lift the boat, so today he'd lower that angle to let the fiberglass set level instead of slipping off at gravity's insistence. A tug at the end of a rope caused the pulley to squeak in protest, but the angle of the hull slowly shifted to level.

Rubbing his palms to temper the rope's sting, he crossed the stern where an odd buckle in the wood planking made him halt in his tracks. There, on the intact end of the original hull, a lump of tape rode the stern like a hidden bomb ready to detonate. Wary, he slipped his phone out of his jeans pocket and took a picture.

A rowdy yowl echoed into the bay. Dalton stepped inside, his gaze scanning the hull. "Okay, what gives in here?"

"Only repair work—until I stumbled onto this tagalong." He gestured at the lump as he put the phone away.

"Whew-dog. That's no barnacle, for sure. Let's take a look-see what it could be."

Perry squared to face his brother. "Just for the record, I had no idea this existed. I found it a mere two seconds before you walked up."

"I'm a believer, take my word for it. Still, only a scarce few items of contraband get that kind of waterproof treatment."

A twinge of pain knifed his side. "Which way do you want to go with this? We can call the sheriff now or take a look for ourselves."

Dalton's expression flinched enough to make his cheek twitch. "Let's take a peek ourselves. We may not need to trouble the sheriff, depending on what we find." In a flash, he slid open his pocketknife and offered possession.

His mouth dry with anticipation, Perry leaned across the hull and raked the knife along one taped edge. After it flopped loose, he scored the adjoining side. Once the third side detached, he pulled the tape free on the final bound edge. Resting the package on the inverted stern, he returned the knife to its owner.

Dalton gave a dry chuckle. "Kinda looks like a personal flotation device, don't it?"

"Yeah, only I'll guess it won't save anybody's life, in this case." He pried his fingers through a gash and ripped the outer wrapper open. Stacks of crisp dollar bills stared back at him, out of place in their humble workshop.

"Wow," Dalton remarked. "Mostly Ben Franklins. You must be holding ten thousand dollars or more."

Worry took on magnified proportions as he began to contemplate the possible repercussions. Though he tried to fold the wrapper back over the bills, it failed to blot out the mockery rife with his find. His stomach roiled. "No, this isn't money. It's pure trouble."

Dalton fished a paper out of his pocket and unfolded it. "Call it double trouble then. Take a look at what Gavin drew late yesterday." He held out the paper for his possession.

The pencil sketch of a sea-going boat with an overhead tow bar filled the paper. "Right, he's got a fixation on boats. We all know that." He gave his brother a skeptical look, unsure of his insinuation.

Dalton tapped the paper at the stern of the boat. "Check out the name."

There, printed across the boat's transom were the letters A-G-U-A, with the G cocked sideways in typical preschooler fashion. "You think Gavin saw Agua Aid in these parts?"

He nodded emphatically. "Right from our dock here on Pantego Creek. Now you tell me what they're doing back here this far from the ocean. It makes no sense whatsoever."

The urge to lose his breakfast came and passed in a flash. When his gaze fell onto the hidden package, his throat filled with gravel. "Agua Aid has been hunting for something in particular—and it all seemed to start the day of my shipwreck."

Dalton cupped his hands on his mouth and blew

a breath into it. "Yeah. Seems like a number of troublesome things got started on the day of your shipwreck."

"What are you trying to say?"

"Better be careful who you trust, that's all. I've got a lot riding on this—and safety of my family is number one."

He glanced up at an array of oil cans that hadn't been moved in thirty years. "Here, you're my witness. I'm stowing this package up on this shelf behind these oil cans for now. When I can make more sense of what's going on, I'll bring the money to the sheriff."

"Don't make me have to do it, Perry," Dalton replied with an edgy tone. "If left for me to bring it in, that likely means something has happened to you. That makes my skin crawl."

He lifted the hefty package and forced it under cover. There, years of grit and dust would guard it well. When he spotted the angst on his kid brother's face, appeasement seemed in order. "I'm not planning to check out early. That wouldn't leave you the chance to call me Old Methuselah when I'm stooped and gray."

A reluctant smile surfaced on his boyish face. "Well, right now you're more of a Jumping Jehoshaphat, but the gray hair is coming, for sure. Just look at Uncle Glenn." He tucked the sketch back into his pocket and put the knife away.

A tiny twist tightened the knot in his side. "Hey, mum's the word to other family members. That's part of keeping them safe."

"Fine, I'll agree to that."

"Good. Now what do you say about lending a hand with this fiberglass so I can get it placed evenly with minimum waste?"

"Man, oh man. I truly hate handling this stuff. It pricks my skin like nothing else."

He started to agree, but decided trouble held a similar texture—prickly and difficult to handle. Instead, he handed Dalton a box of fiberglass strips, unable to avoid the inevitable contact. A reliable division between a man and the sea forestalled the next calamity. For the first time, making a living hovered over a depthless body of water made less sense. "Maybe we'll go double thickness to insure the waterproof seal." Even with Dalton's nod, it seemed a thin trust.

~

Two hours into the transect research, Jaima realized the ghost crabs had indeed migrated up into the more stable primary dunes. Now out of hurricane season, November only brought linear winds to shift the sands around. Still, a little burrow maintenance never bothered a crustacean. As a tangential thought, maybe she would extend the transect zone into the secondary dunes to discover if its expanded territory offered equal protection as prime habitat.

Before she could make a notation in her logbook, a Suburban marked with the sheriff's department seal bucked across the metal ramp of the dune crossover and headed down to cape pointe. *Odd mix.* Never in her uncountable days on the beach had she seen law enforcement breach the pavement barrier to make an austere presence on the shore.

The illusion of possessing a haven from such intrusion shattered as the sea oats clicked together in the wind. Marking the date in her logbook, she started to note the expansion concept stated as a null hypothesis that the ghost crabs would not prefer the secondary dune. When she glanced up, blue lights churned in revolutions on the sheriff's roof, turning the seawater off cape pointe to hopeless gray by immediate comparison.

An encounter ensued, but she stood too far away to make out any details. As the vehicle headed back to the crossover, she feigned interest in her fieldwork to avoid any direct gaze. The SUV passed less than twenty feet away from her upper transect. When she glanced over, she caught Monte's frozen gaze in the mirror, his face stern like the fated old man and the sea. Cape pointe grew inhospitable, too cold to bear. She tucked away her notes to head in for a hot lunch.

Chapter 8

Even in foul weather, the wealthy wore the embossment of finery, the best money could buy. Perry tried not to let his disposition sour, as two of the three fishing hotspots Dalton maneuvered through produced a multitude of catches for the pharmaceutical group. A brisk north wind made them keep their fancy outerwear zipped for full protection. He'd ignore the logos that spoke of designer labels with hefty price tags. A short man fumbled his flounder over the gunwale and made a wisecrack about its flat face.

He grabbed the pliers to remove the fisherman's hook and recalled Jaima's advice to look for deeper meaning in the encounter today. "Hey, there's nothing wrong with doing everything in your power to look up." He pointed skyward with the pliers to reinforce his meaning.

The man laughed instead of answering. His buddy opened a nearby cooler to accept the addition. Minus the tethering hook, the flat fish belly-flopped into the container.

Perry wiped his hands down his jeans and glanced over at Dalton's boat. Two men reeled in bent poles, actively catching fish. He'd let the two boats drift closer so they could plan out the closing hour. Since the tour group scheduled an evening fish fry at Wrights Creek Boat Access, maybe a trip around the cusp of Stumpy Point would be in order. That habitat spiel might be just what the drug-makers needed. If Limulus came up a time or two in conversation, he'd consider that downright providential.

A second glance at Dalton yielded the sign he wanted. One clap over his head signaled time to move out. He stepped behind the helm of his uncle's boat, more than ready to let the tour group face the music for marine conservation. After all, blood was thicker than water. In this unique case for tapping horseshoe crabs, both were blue. When the pools of Jaima's blue eyes crossed his minds-eye, the perfect trifecta fell unmistakable. He revved the engine with a thrust of throttle, causing the Pharma fishermen to clutch the railing for support, a sign of weakness that paid the instant dividend of confidence for the captain.

~

The director stormed her office and took the guest chair, unusual for a Monday morning. Jaima turned away from her computer screen to lend her full attention. "Good morning, Fran. I hope you had a nice weekend."

"Maybe too short," the director replied, "if you know what I mean."

Since she hadn't been invited out to Belhaven, her weekend had seemed interminable. She understood the two-boat charter took precedence, but a late phone call would have been nice. Hands folded, she drew upon some professional forbearance. "Go ahead, Fran."

She unfolded a newspaper with drama. "Did you see this? First, Terry Bonner's boat goes up in flames, and then *he* goes missing for five days. I'm quite concerned for his well-being. You know Terry's been a patron member for fifteen years."

Uncomfortable with the disclosure, she took the paper and skimmed the article. From all appearances, their loyal member was allegedly entangled in some kind of smuggling scheme. At the close of the article, the reporter confirmed the involvement of the FBI. "Good grief. I probably watched him head out to fish a hundred times this summer. All I saw was his little blue boat puttering by, not some diabolical smuggling venture underway."

"Some things are not what they seem. I came in to ask you a specific question. Have you heard any hints of how the aquarium might be involved? I reflect back to our touch tank incident, where it seems a perpetrator intended us harm for a reason I cannot figure out."

Her mouth fell open at the mild insinuation. "Uh, no—not in the least. That tampering act may have been a juvenile prank and totally unrelated."

The director stood and brushed the wrinkles from her slacks. "Perhaps not unrelated, Jaima. I also came in to tell you the back exit by your Limulus Lab received damage over the weekend, but the deadbolt held. Whoever tried to infiltrate the facility failed to gain access. I'm calling the mayor next to see what he can do to better insure our safety. I plan to request an hourly patrol through the circular parking lot."

She stood to better regard her boss eye to eye. "I commend that action. And a safety meeting with staff might be in order. It's been a while since we reviewed protocol addressing a suspicious act, or how to preserve a crime scene."

Fran popped her skinny black glasses into place. "I have no intention of this aquarium becoming the scene of any crime. As the old saying goes, knowledge replaces fear. I'll not cower while some ne'er-do-well tries to turn our educational facility into his backdrop for misadventure."

"You have my full support, Director Michaels. No one has more to lose than I do. That Limulus Lab took me months to establish."

She started to exit, pulling the door closed behind her. With only a crack left ajar, she peered back inside. "I recall that you showed your gentleman friend the research lab only two weeks ago. Be careful who you trust, Jaima. The kiss of a friend stings more than the embrace of an enemy." The door pulled closed to end the exchange.

Jaima sank in her seat, her posture rigid from the break-in news. Yes, she had toured Perry back there as a diversion, though he had nothing to gain. Ill at ease, she examined every seam of their friendship to expose any disingenuous gap. Her reflections left her on the beach, the two of them alternating the catch of bluefish like some synchrony of divine fate. He'd kissed her for the first time that afternoon, until Monte passed by and the fish needed cleaning.

She hung her head as distrust leaked onto tender heartstrings. "Why, oh why, does life on the coast always have to smell like rotten fish?" Edwina's rendering of growing tired of the wave-slapped shore drove a seed of discontent into her off-balanced Monday. On impulse, she rose to go check the horseshoe crabs using the wet lab in the research wing to grow toward their next molt of maturity. *Protect the innocent, Lord.* As her heels clicked down the hall, she tried not to feel like a traitor, offering them up as replacement bleeders once their time arrived.

~

"The next step is up to us," Perry said, his gaze skittering from his brother to his uncle. The tavern's dim lighting made the gathering feel illegal. Though Aunt Peggy wouldn't approve, the bar served the biggest burger platters in town.

Dalton rubbed a knuckle across the shellacked table. "Really, we stood shoulder to shoulder with these fellas cleaning their fish, and the topic of adding a coastal facility just popped up. The chief manager said they'd been contemplating a separate lab for the marine life and said it made total sense to base that part on the coast. I think their interest is legit."

Uncle Glenn propped an elbow on the table. "You didn't mention our fifty-five acres specifically, did you?"

"No, sir," Perry replied. "We have to be in agreement within the family first. I'm sure several properties exist around Belhaven that would suit their needs and possess good highway access for transport, but we own waterfront."

"Which is rare," Dalton interjected. "They would pay well for that kind of access to the open sea."

Glenn fidgeted, looking plenty uncomfortable. "What about the chance of pollution? We don't want to invite trouble to Belhaven."

Perry shook his head. "They run a green star facility, and the management is pretty proud of their clean environmental track record."

"It's our land deal," Dalton insisted. "If we want some type of quality control for the creek, we could write that into the contract."

Perry pressed his fingertips into prayer position. "As best I can tell, this setup would match well with what Jaima is trying to accomplish at the aquarium—a bank for investing in horseshoe crabs. The pharmaceutical company could partner with the aquarium and cooperate instead of being at odds. That's the solution that holds the most promise."

When a waitress approached with laden platters, Glenn threw up his hands. "I concede to make the offer to the pharmaceutical company—but I want to set the asking price."

Perry took one look at the juicy burger dripping with melted cheese and trusted they had embarked on the right course. "I can give you the manager's business card tonight."

"No, you're going to make that call." Glenn paused to allow his platter to be served. "I'll phone you tonight with my figure, and I want you to make the offer tomorrow."

"Then I'd better pray over these burgers," he replied. "There's nothing like being on God's good side before wandering into unknown territory." Grace came more heartfelt with that admission. He even mentioned giving back instead of constantly taking from the sea. The shift lent him inner peace. He opened his eyes to find Dalton stealing a french fry off his plate. *Typical filching prank.* That kind of minor loss he could withstand. Hopefully, Jaima would be on board for the rest of his plan.

~

Paranoia had set in at work, turning the aquarium adversarial. Jaima welcomed a quiet Thursday evening at home as she pulled into the apartment complex. With all the parking spots filled, she ended up further toward the end of the building than usual. Activity down by the dumpster caught her attention where she spied a team of uniformed officers picking out trash. *What's that about?* A prickle of unease crossed the back of her neck, causing her hairs to stand.

A man dressed in gray approached from the stairwell. "Miss Delarie? I'd like to ask you a few questions about Monte Creef, if you have a few minutes to spare."

She faked a smile. "Sorry. I don't talk to strangers."

He reached into his jacket and produced an ID badge. "Walker Grantham with the FBI. As you know, I investigated the boat burning down at the marina. I believe we met that day, did we not?"

From his rigid stance, she knew not to kid around. "We didn't formally meet, Mr. Grantham, but as I recall, you did take my picture."

"That's right. I did. We are detaining your friend Monte Creef in conjunction with that act of arson."

Indignation rose from deep in her chest. "That's insane. Monte was fishing out on cape pointe. The sheriff drove out there to arrest him. He couldn't have torched that boat."

The man drew out a pad and jotted down a note. "Are you aware that Terry Bonner and Monte Creef are first cousins?"

The implication stung. "I—no. I had no knowledge of their kinship." Though trying to remain stone-faced, Edwina popped to mind. With enough troubles of her own, the old woman would be the last name she would offer. "Are you implying the two cousins were somehow in collusion for this alleged smuggling ring reported in the newspaper?"

"Yes, I am more than implying. I have substantial evidence of their cooperative venture." He leaned closer as if to appear more formidable. "What kind of smuggling is going on, Miss Delarie? Would you like to show any of your cards? It might serve you well later in court."

She shrugged, swallowing down her ire. "I'm sorry. I thought you were going to tell me, Mr. Grantham. I'm not a conduit for illegal activity. I'm a researcher at the local aquarium. I have no foreknowledge of your smuggling ring and thus sleep with a clean conscious at night."

While he jotted another note, two officers approached, clutching a bag between them. "Here's the stash, just like you predicted," the taller man said.

Before she could ask her next question, a truck pulled into the parking lot and nosed into the scene. She glanced through the windshield to see Perry staring wide-eyed at the situation. "What kind of setup are you trying to pull on me?" she posed in a low voice to the agent.

Perry slid from behind the wheel and came to stand beside her.

Grantham held up his palm for silence and flashed the badge for Perry's benefit. He yanked at the cinch strap and opened the trash bag, which spread a stench that made the bearer gag. He gestured inside the sack. "This illegally-harvested marine life is being sold to pharmaceutical companies while raking designated sanctuaries bare. We've had similar cases up and down the Atlantic seaboard, so we recognized the signs right away. None of these fisheries' actions are permitted, and charges will be filed. Due to your possession of this contraband material, Miss Delarie, I'm inviting you downtown for further questioning."

Perry shoved in front like a human guard. "You're off base. Jaima is totally innocent."

The agent chuckled while nodding to the officers to take possession. "No need to play the superhero, Mr. Manning. Yes, we know who you are, but haven't found any tangible link for your involvement, so enjoy your freedom—for now."

Afraid to even breathe, Jaima followed his gesture and let the policemen lead to their patrol car. After being seated, she regarded the world from an unyielding wire-mesh cage, not unlike the glass walls of an aquarium, a total entrapment. Before the door could clamp closed, she spied Perry stooped by the rear fender.

"Re-examine your loyalties," he insisted, his expression stern.

"It starts and ends with Limulus." She shook her head as the door slammed shut, and off they went toward interrogation central, hidden deep within a tranquil island paradise.

Chapter 9

Jaima shifted in her desk chair, uncomfortable with the forced end to her work week. Everything she once held as noble sat corrupted by the FBI agent's interrogation report. Negative fallout included being placed on probation at the aquarium, an undeserved tarnish on her professional career ordered by the Board of Directors in an emergency meeting held last night. Her love of fishing brought this demise which now demoted her favorite pastime into the history book of prior endeavors. Maybe the hospital's thrift store would accept her donation of a dozen surf rods cluttering up her storage area at the apartment.

The office door creaked open. Fran approached with two coffee cups in her hands. "Hey. I thought making a second pot this afternoon might serve us both like good medicine. Please join me." She sat and offered one cup across the desk blotter with a faint smile.

Jaima sensed a glimmer of friendship in the offer so she accepted the cup. "I'll take mine black to match my inner gloom."

"Oh, that's dark commentary for a Friday." She

slid to the front of the chair and pulled something from under her suit jacket's lapel. "This came in today's mail for you—from the state House of Representatives."

Though hardly in the mood for political rhetoric, she accepted the envelope and tore it open. Her gaze dropped to the handwritten signature and note by her state representative. "Okay, here goes nothing. 'Dear Ms. Delarie, After corroborating your account of establishing the national memorial commemorating the site of first flight, the State of North Carolina hereby deems the reparation to the Creef family overdue and lack of payment inexcusable by a public entity. Under the authority granted me as state representative of Dare County, I hereby offer this two-fold reparation supported by the Community Civility Endowment as the following.

"First, a monetary payment of two thousand five hundred dollars is to be made to the matriarch of the Creef family, Edwina Creef, or her designee, for labor performed to create the monument hill heretofore unremitted since the year nineteen hundred and three. Secondly, as a tribute to previously unheralded local citizenry's efforts to construct this historic monument, the access road around the pinnacle statue formerly known as Monument Drive shall be renamed Creef Circle and properly noted by coordinating signage. Thank you for bringing this historic omission to my attention. Note the reparation check will be forthcoming, sent in your care for bequeathal to the Creef family. Most sincerely, Albert Hoffling, Public Servant.'"

"Well, I'll be," Fran said. "Justice comes in many forms, and sometimes it arrives right in the nick of time."

Some of the heaviness lifted from Jaima's heart and she sat a bit straighter at her desk. "I'm speechless, Fran. I thought my meek request had a snowball's chance beside hell's blazing furnace."

The director gazed down into her cup as if it held a dose of wisdom. "Jaima, hear me out. I don't think your career ends in disarray here at the aquarium. Your research capabilities are visionary, no matter the setting. I want you to consider going back to the university and rededicating your passion to a new line of research."

"But what about the horseshoe crabs in Limulus Lab?"

"We have a new grad student starting in January for the spring semester. Let's give him the lab and let him run with it. That's called empowerment for the next generation of researchers. Feel free to write down procedures and label the lab stations to make the transition more workable. You've had an outstanding five years here, but you're ready for more of a challenge. Please consider my suggestion and put some inquiries out there."

She held her face in her hands trying to steady a bad case of jitters. Affiliation with the aquarium had served as her anchor, and now her director requested relocation to a different port. Still, Fran's loyalty and support represented a consistent part of her tenure there. Maybe she had a blind spot her mentor could spot more readily than she could. "Okay, let me contact a few department heads and check on what might be available. Coming into the facility at the middle of the school year might prove problematic."

"Or some professor could be in a tight spot and need capable backup support. In that light, you could be an answer to prayer. You certainly were an answer to mine."

She dropped one hand onto the letter and rubbed the gold seal embossing the letterhead. "Thanks for the reminder that God has a plan for me—not for my harm, but for my good."

Fran rose, the slight smile returning. "Every pivot starts the next move forward. I'll go write you a letter of highest recommendation, the least I can do to aid your pending transition." She gave a musical hum and departed.

Jaima dropped her gaze to the congressional resolution again and read back through its terms. At the conclusion, she felt a compelling urge to visit Edwina with the reparation news. She couldn't drive directly there from the aquarium for risk of being followed. A better plan came to mind. Early Saturday morning, she would pick up fresh donuts at the bakery and deliver tasty sweets with the remarkable revelation. *Good timing for encouraging news.* Maybe the old woman would soften enough to let her clean the house a little to disinfect the heaving shanty that needed salvation as much as its owner did.

~

Working late on the boat repair helped cover the sore issue Perry still needed to address. With no word from Jaima since the scene at her apartment, his plea for examining loyalties may have dealt a toxic blow to their relationship. In it too deep to properly sort matters out, he let time slip by, his typical passive recourse. He reached for the epoxy, ready to mix up the next batch which, ironically, covered the spot where the money stash had been affixed. Who knew his friendly solicitation for spare gas that ill-fated day at sea would have led to such treachery?

Dalton stepped into the workshop bay, trailed by Beth. "Excuse us, Perry. Hold up a short minute. We need to talk."

He shoved the epoxy tube back into the carton. "Go ahead little brother. What's on your mind this evening?"

Dalton toed some shavings on the floor, looking bashful. "Beth and I talked it over. Having that cash on hand is a magnet for trouble where we least can handle any. It's high time we bring that parcel to the authorities and tell them what we know about Agua Aid."

"Do you mean our presumption that wouldn't fill a thimble?"

"No," Beth replied. "But they're hot to find something, Perry, and you discovered a cache worth locating, so put two and two together."

Dalton stepped closer. "I think we may need to go over the sheriff's head with this. You know that FBI agent's on assignment in Manteo. We should take the stash to him."

"They guy who practically threw Jaima in jail? No, you're asking too much."

"Dalton will go with you," Beth said. "He can

testify about the rough encounter at Wrights Creek Boat Access. Plus, he can show them Gavin's sketch."

The sudden tug on his inertia felt like an outgoing tide, full of scour and abrasion. How much safer would it be if he could stay hidden like the money and wait out the high drama? Having his passivity exposed under the spotlight grew uncomfortable. "No, I vote we wait."

"Until what?" Beth's voice pressed in a gentle tone. "One of the boys is approached? Or possibly taken? Put yourself in my shoes, Perry. I can't stand guard twenty-four hours a day."

Dalton extended his palm. "I'll go with you, bro. Two Mannings make a mighty strong fortress. Plus, we can have each other's backs. Let's leave for Manteo police station at nine o'clock tomorrow morning."

He glanced over at the oil can shelf and noticed one corner of the cash package still exposed in plain sight. A rookie at behind-the-scenes activity, maybe it *was* the right time to come forward. "Okay, but let's leave at eight-thirty instead. I want to be there right when they open for walk-in traffic."

"There goes my beauty sleep," Dalton teased with a fake grimace.

"We'll go to bed early," Beth added. "The boys and I will stay busy making decorations for our Thanksgiving celebration. Gratitude always starts in the heart."

Perry took his brother's hand and gave it a hearty shake. "No wonder you keep her around, Dalton. Meet me at the truck at eight-thirty—or I'll hunt you down."

"Don't make me show off my Scooby Doo pajamas in town," Dalton quipped. "No worries, I'll be ready."

As his family departed, Perry made a protracted inspection of the hull repair. Smooth and flawless on the outside, he knew damage existed deeper inside. With that kind of splintered frame, a fisherman ran the risk of not being seaworthy. *Weak spot, for sure.* Why his thoughts shifted to Jaima upon that recognition, he hadn't a clue. Dejected at his inability to bring any resolution, he grabbed the money stash and flicked off the shop light, heading inside for a late bite to eat and possibly some rest, God willing.

Chapter 10

Of all days to sleep late, today proved most unfortunate. Jaima hurried from downtown, realizing the restoration work had already begun with her attitude. Late last night, she'd decided the aquarium didn't represent her end-all. Projecting forward held a slight thrill. She had e-mailed two inquiries to separate universities for possible research work, thus taking the first steps for the pivot. The aroma of powdered sugar sweetened the SUV's interior as she eased to the curb in front of Edwina's house and turned off the ignition.

After pulling out the box of goodies, she noticed the newspapers piling up across the street at the base of Monte's driveway. Regret thickened her throat as she scampered up the broken concrete walkway. Her fishing friend had chosen a dark path of his own accord—presuming he'd be found guilty. At any rate, the matriarch of the Creef family deserved some respect and a bit of companionship. The letter in her back pocket would likely produce tears of joy. She would bring the good news to bear at the ideal time and pause to savor the moment.

Edwina shuffled to the front door and peered out

the screen. "I declare. It's our 'quarium girl paying me a visit on a gloomy day. Come right on in."

Hope filled her lungs as she inhaled the crisp autumn air. "I'm not much in the mood for waves slapping the shore today, so I thought a chat might cheer up both of us."

"I like the way you think." She popped open the door latch and beckoned her inside.

"I sure hope you haven't eaten yet. I brought donuts from Maddie's Bakery."

"I claim the cinnamon twist, if you picked up one."

A true conspirator, Jaima nudged her host's bony shoulder as she stepped inside. "I picked two up—one for both of us." She followed the time-bent woman as she headed for the back room, the aroma of brewing coffee hanging in the air like a lure for friends to conspire.

~

At the agent's insistence, Perry sat at Full Sails Marina, his brother perched on the front bumper as bait to attract his old football nemesis at Agua Aid. Something about the smuggling ring didn't make a complete circle in his reasoning until Grantham mentioned a suspicious link with the sea tow outfit. If they were looking for payment money left by Terry Bonner under the hull of his boat, that would confirm the company's involvement.

Four undercover officers waited down on the docks in case the men tried to flee. To maintain authenticity, the police had asked the marina owners to make a subtle presence in and out of the office on the north dock. With seagulls crying overhead, it had the makings of a typical Saturday on the coast—though layers deeper, the day resembled anything but normal. Having no stomach for spy work, his gut churned with mounting tension.

Looking every bit the retired running back, Dalton lifted his cap to flag an approaching vehicle. He reached behind his shoulder and gave the hood a knock, their secret signal the plot unfolded as planned. One arm extended straight out meant he needed help pronto.

Two men walked up the sidewalk along the dock's planking. Perry recognized them both from Wrights Creek, so maybe they represented the two main players. Not far below, a plain-clothes officer moved up the dock, swishing a damp mop back and forth. A pelican took wing off a post at their approach.

"Hey, Carlos," Dalton called. "Thanks for coming out this morning."

"No problem, dude—especially if you have that gift pack you promised."

Perry recognized his cue and opened the truck door, lifting the money cache in sight. He stepped beside his brother, assuming the lead. "I ran my boat aground on cape pointe the day your shipment went missing. I didn't realize that while I poured gas from his spare jug, Terry Bonner transferred the money cache to my boat. I think you guys might have been expecting that payoff, right?" Though he tried to remain casual, the agent's insistence of getting that link-up confessed might be crucial for the case later in court. Dread began to make his knees shake.

Carlos laughed, his brown eyes intense. "Let's just call that an indirect hike bypassing the quarterback, man. Looks like the running back and his brother have the goods, so what matters is the payola gets delivered to the rightful owner—us. If you just hand the package over nice and easy, nobody takes a penalty."

"Fine," Perry replied with a nod. "That's what we intend to do. Believe me, we sure don't plan to keep it." He extended the bulging package.

Carlos took it with a greedy snatch. He flipped past the outer wrapper and stuck his fingers into the wad of bills. A smile spread across his ruddy face. "Looks good, my friend."

Grantham flashed his badge while running toward the intercept. "Hold it right there, gentlemen."

When Carlos started to flee, Dalton leapt from the truck's bumper to grab him but the quick-moving accomplice blocked his efforts. Under a full-out pinning, Dalton managed to send him the straight arm help signal.

Angered at the thought of a possible escape from justice, Perry's inertia shattered. Rocketed into a heated chase along the upper docks, he lunged at the smuggler, wrapped his legs in a full tackle, and held on tight until Grantham could take over. Within moments, two police officers clamped down and gained custody of Carlos, standing him up to face the agent.

Grantham took possession of the money cache while two more officers appeared dragging the accomplice along and clamped on handcuffs. The

FBI agent shouldered between them in a power move. "Tell us who your connection is to Monte Creef and Terry Bonner. If you cooperate now, I'll make a note of it in my report." His scowl seemed to amplify the request.

"Those guys just do the collecting," the antsy accomplice blurted. "The big boss goes by Eddie."

Carlos kicked the man's shin and cocked his head. His dark eyes seethed with disdain.

Dizzy from the physical confrontation, Perry leaned back on the truck's hood and shaded his eyes from the late morning sun. At least he'd gotten rid of the ill-fated stash. *Talk about the wrong kind of money.*

While the officers rough-handled the men toward their patrol cars, Dalton joined him. "Do you know who this Eddie could be?" His eyebrows rose with the inquiry.

Perry glanced between his innocent kid brother and the pushy federal agent. "No, I don't. Edwina is the only other Creef I know. The old woman and Jaima have been tight friends a while. In fact, Jaima takes her trash periodically and disposes of it in the apartment dumpster as a thoughtful act of kindness."

"We're going to pay old Edwina a visit," Grantham said. "Can you lead the way?"

A lump formed in his throat, as the visit had all the makings of a betrayal. "I only know where Monte lives, but Edwina supposedly lives right across the street."

"Since we need to maintain the element of surprise, we're going over straight from here,"

Grantham replied. "No phone calls."

Perry swallowed his objection and returned to the cab. He keyed the ignition and waited for the passenger door to slam before throwing the gear shift into reverse. Too bad he couldn't back up the entire route. That's the kind of begrudged cooperation Grantham deserved.

"Remember what you told Jaima," Dalton said in a timid tone. "Re-examine your loyalties, bro. The upright road always proves the right trail in the end."

"Still, this kind of betrayal cuts a deep rut in the sand. Jaima probably won't ever speak to me again after all this clears. One thing's for sure—I know she's not involved in the smuggling scheme." Resolute to prove it, he crossed the bridge beside the marina making the water below ripple with jumping minnows. *Always fish involved.* He jammed the gas pedal in a silent dare for the agent to match his pace.

~

Jaima watched the sparkle return to the old woman's eyes and soaked in the glorious moment that had taken over a century to transpire. She nibbled the last bite of her second donut and savored fate's sweet juncture. For the briefest duration, life had turned good again.

"Read me that part about the road naming again," Edwina insisted. Her gnarled hands clasped the worn mug that held the last dregs of her milked-down coffee. "The overdue money payment may be one thing, but I declare, that road naming is something else."

She held the letter to her chest. "That's my favorite part, too. For all days to come, people will see the Creef name affiliated with the Wright Brothers Memorial. That makes my spirit soar. I know you must be proud."

She nodded and her thin white hair shook. "Plenty proud enough for me and for my grandpa, too. Maybe you could take my picture beside it when they put up the new road sign."

She sipped her lukewarm coffee to clear powdered sugar from her throat. "You bet I will. What a sight that's gonna be." She adjusted the letter into reading position, but before she could read the entry, a hammering knock shook the front door. "Oh, are you expecting any other company this morning?"

Edwina shook her head. Worry snuffed out the newfound sparkle in her gray eyes. "No, not that I know of."

"You stay put. I'll go get the door." She rose and made the wander through the central hallway into the front room. To her amazement, Perry stood at the screen door. Not too delighted at the intrusion, she feigned politeness and opened the door. "Hey. What gives?"

"I need to see Edwina. Is she home?" He rubbed one fist into one palm, as if he had something tangible to offer but had come up empty-handed.

"Just a minute. I'll see if she's willing to take another caller this morning. We've been celebrating some good news. The reparation came in for the Creef family yesterday. They're getting payment and a road named for the family around the Wright

Brothers Memorial."

"That's incredibly nice," he replied in a gravelly voice.

A commotion ensued from the rear of the house. Edwina's outburst of objection gave her prickles down her back. "What's going on, Perry?"

He spread his stance. "Edwina was identified by the Agua Aid crew as the mastermind in the smuggling ring marketing marine life for cash. We set up a trap for their crew this morning and she surfaced as the link. I'm so sorry it fell out like this, Jaima. Please accept my apology."

Grantham came through the front room, forcing Edwina forward with a tight grip on the old woman's bony arm. "Let's head down to the police station, Mr. Manning. I think Miss Creef might have some confessing to do."

When Perry opened the door, Jaima stepped out first. A fount of held-back indignation erupted. She fired off a seething look his way. "Of all the unmitigated gall. What a Judas you proved to be. Thanks for nothing."

Grantham shoved through the doorway, drawing Edwina outside. "That's the unbiased arm of the law, Ms. Delarie. Friend or not, justice must be upheld. Who's going to put those illegally-harvested marine animals back in their habitats? All are lost, just to be ground up for some memory-enhancement pills pushed by the pharmaceutical companies."

As the smuggling ring's motivation fell into place, awareness of how large her blind spot had grown engulfed her, stealing her next breath. Even the nonprofit aquarium couldn't keep mal-intent from occurring, especially when greed drove the fishing boat. Habitat conservation always battled unchecked human consumption, a realization that carried a potent sting.

"Excuse me, officer," Edwina said in a shaky voice. "Could you let me go grab my cane? Otherwise, all this walking will be next to impossible for me." She squirmed loose of his hold and headed back inside.

Perry stepped closer, crowding her on the porch. "Listen, Jaima. I tried to warn you about your loyalties. Monte had little involvement, as it turns out. Terry Bonner was the main supplier. If guilty in part, I still think we can angle to get Monte some time off for cooperating."

Her mind began to swirl with implications of a legal trial and guilt split among family members. With her head swimming, the front porch began to tilt and her knees soon buckled. Two strong arms kept her from hitting the planking as Perry nestled her into his side. After a few dull-witted moments, the old woman's ruse struck home. Chills crept down her spine. "Wait a second. Edwina doesn't use a cane."

Grantham rushed through the door as gun blast echoed from the rear of the house. In a matter of seconds, he reappeared, shaking his head while reaching for his phone. Two police cars drifted to the curb, their flashing lights elevating the new state of emergency.

Perry pulled her into the crook of his neck. "Take heart, Jaima. At least you gave Edwina the satisfaction of the reparation news. That counts for mending the generational family rift."

She instantly regretted that the reparation arrived so late for her friend, barely on time. A hot tear streaked down her cheek, soon followed by a steady stream. "We'll bury her at low tide on the Creef family plot in Buxton. I'll carry a lantern and lead the children, just like in Edwina's story of her grandparents' burial."

Perry held her tighter. "That sounds highly honoring. Count on me to be there."

An ambulance screamed upon approach, lifting her thoughts from mortal loss to a higher plain of life continued. Stalwart at her side, her fishing friend persisted to stake a claim for future involvement which somehow buoyed her faltering spirit. She took a few precious moments to grieve the old woman's passing. The taste of tears made her feel alive, a salt-stung heritage wrought from living threateningly close to the incessant ocean.

Epilogue

The open gazebo at the cemetery's perimeter offered little protection from December's biting wind. Perry zipped up his jacket until the fastener poked his neck. He fixed his gaze on Jaima as she tucked plastic flowers into the base of the new Creef headstone. The federal reparation money ended up embossing the family's name in granite, a fitting end.

Jaima turned to face him. "Tell me what you think the headstone looks like,"

"It resembles two waves crashing together to make one." The ocean analogy might earn him some brownie points. When she smiled, he knew he'd succeeded. "Hey, come sit with me a few minutes. I have some breaking news straight from Belhaven."

She returned to the gazebo. "I didn't realize anything moved fast enough in Belhaven to merit breaking news." She slid onto the bench beside him and adjusted her wool scarf.

"After we made buddies with that pharmaceutical outfit from Charlotte on the fishing tour, first one thing led to another regarding a coastal field lab to process the marine life in a more humane way. Uncle Glenn offered them a fifty-five acre tract left by my grandfather, and the company bought it last week. They hope to do a quick-build on the site using a Morton building frame-up so the lab facility can be underway by springtime."

Her gaze searched his face. "Are you serious?"

"Totally serious. In the purchase contract, Dalton helped me write a few environmental protection clauses so they have to manage their outputs to Pantego Creek, plus guard the viability of any animals used for research, including the horseshoe crab."

"Including Limulus?" Her question held a slight falter.

Now he approached the truth of the matter, whether she might envision being involved or not. "You could establish Limulus Lab Number Two, if you want to take part in this operation." With a tiny ounce of encouragement, he would sweeten the deal.

"And work in the private sector…plus live in Belhaven?" Creases worked her brow into a knot. "But I wouldn't be able to hear the waves slap the shore from there."

"Consider how refreshing it could be to live inland. I confess your Director Michaels thought the idea held enough merit that she forwarded her letter of recommendation to our contact at the pharmaceutical company earlier this week."

She took a handful of hair and wove it around the scarf. "Guess I would still live near the water in a sense."

Her receptivity prompted him to reveal his heart. "Jaima, Belhaven welcomes you with open arms." As he spread his palms, he dropped to his knees. "One additional part of the offer goes like this. My life hasn't been the same since the shipwreck when you dragged me from the ocean. Instead of dying that day, I came alive in a way I'd never dreamed possible—a man full of love for a remarkable woman. If you're even willing to entertain the job offer in Belhaven, I'd like you to consider a nobler proposal—one from my heart. Would you marry me and love me through all time? I want to have a beautiful life together with you." An afterthought, he pulled out the velvet box and displayed the diamond ring. "This is my mother's ring, which I now ask you to wear as my beloved wife."

Her eyes misted as she nodded. "Yes. How wonderful for us to find each other despite all this tragedy."

He slid the ring on her finger to solidify his proposal. "And so it doesn't go unsaid, when you marry a fisherman, there's always going to be plenty of fish nearby." From the way she clutched his neck tighter, he considered that a seal of assurance their bond would last the test of time. "Got 'em on, kept 'em on," he teased before landing a kiss on her salty lips. Her tender consent felt like having his boat run with the tide at long last, the ultimate act of cooperation for a land-dweller attempting to stay afloat.

The End

SALT STUNG ON CAPE HATTERAS

AUTHOR BIO

A coastal North Carolina native, Cindy M. Amos writes fiction about conflicts of man living on the land. Holding an advanced degree in coastal marine biology, she researched the dynamic outer shoreline that keeps the mighty Atlantic Ocean off the mainland with a mere spit of sand. Weaving nature's intricate physical processes with the flaw-prone human influences prevalent in beachfront living, she calls a truce between resource overuse and coastal heritage. Like the heroine Jaima, her first job in grad school involved measuring the population of ghost crabs living on the beach at Salvo and Hatteras. In this novel, threads of truth reveal unfinished business regarding establishment of the Wright Brothers National Memorial, an element straight out of the author's family history. Proud to have stood in the shore break when the bluefish ran the perilous inlet at Cape Hatteras, Ms. Amos offers this story of unexpected romance, betrayed loyalties, and unresolved failures recurring on the fringe of islands bordering the Graveyard of the Atlantic.

"Salt-Stung on Cape Hatteras" represents the author's 40th book with Editor Cynthia Hickey at Winged Publications, a small traditional publisher out of Surprise, Arizona.

Member: American Christian Fiction Writers and Heart of America Christian Writers Network.

Her entire booklist with Winged Publications can be found on her website:
http://cindymamos.wixsite.com/natureink

Her author page on Amazon is found at:
https://www.amazon.com/Cindy-M.-Amos

~Writing romance onto nature's landscape~

OTHER BOOKS BY CINDY M. AMOS
Landscapes of Mercy Series
Redeeming River Rancher
Saving Bicycle Man
Justifying Sound Strider
Sanctifying Ace Aerialist
Lifting Lock Runner
Salvaging Doctor Junk

National Parks 100th Anniversary
Romance Collection
Everglades Entanglement
Mesa Verde Meltdown

Holiday 3-in-1 Collection
Running Out of Christmastime

Taming the Cowboy's Heart Collection
Warming Stone Cold Lodge

50 States Collection
Secondhand Flower Stand (Kansas)
Red Cloud Retreat (Nebraska)
Tidewater Lowlands (North Carolina)
Canyon Country Courtship (Utah)

John Denver 20th Anniversary Collection
Calypso Reimagined

Loving the Town Hero Collection
Cascading Waterworks

Cowboy Brides Collection
Renegade Restoration

America's Fabulous Fifties Series
Oil Field Maven
Airfield Aptitude
Camp Field Capable

Small Town Christmas Collection 2018
Gift Tag Tree

Romancing the Rancher's Daughter Collection
Waylaying the Hauler

Romancing the Farmer Collection
Furrowed Hearts

Adventure Brides Collection
Ocean's Edge

Romancing the Bachelor Collection
Impasse to Springtime

Romancing the Boy Next Door Collection
Forty Acres on Loan

Romancing the Doctor Collection
X-Raying the Doctor

Vote for Love Collection
Ballot Box Rumors

A Secret Santa Romance Collection
Sweet Regrets from Sourwood

Christmas Cookie Brides Collection
Pizzelles for Elves

Romancing the Drifter Collection
Derailing the Drifter

A Family to Love Collection
Skinny Ranch Romance

Nonfiction Little Lift Gift Books
Signs of the Seasons: Hints from Nature

The Men of Mustang Pass Series
Silver Lining at Mustang Pass
Copper Halo at Mustang Pass
Sapphire Skies at Mustang Pass
Holiday Hitches at Mustang Pass

Horizons of Hidden Promise
Rekindled from Ashes
Reconciled from Heartache

Made in the USA
Monee, IL
23 September 2021